Created by Pendleton Ward

Written by **Ashly Burch**

Illustrated by **Diigii Daguna**

Colors by **Braden Lamb**

Letters by **Warren Montgomery**

Cover by **Braden Lamb & Shelli Paroline**

"Fish Days"
Written & Illustrated by Marina Julia

Designer **Grace Park**
Associate Editor **Whitney Leopard**
Editor **Shannon Watters**

With Special Thanks to Marisa Marionakis, Janet No, Nicole Rivera, Conrad Montgomery, Meghan Bradley, Curtis Lelash, Kelly Crews and the wonderful folks at Cartoon Network.

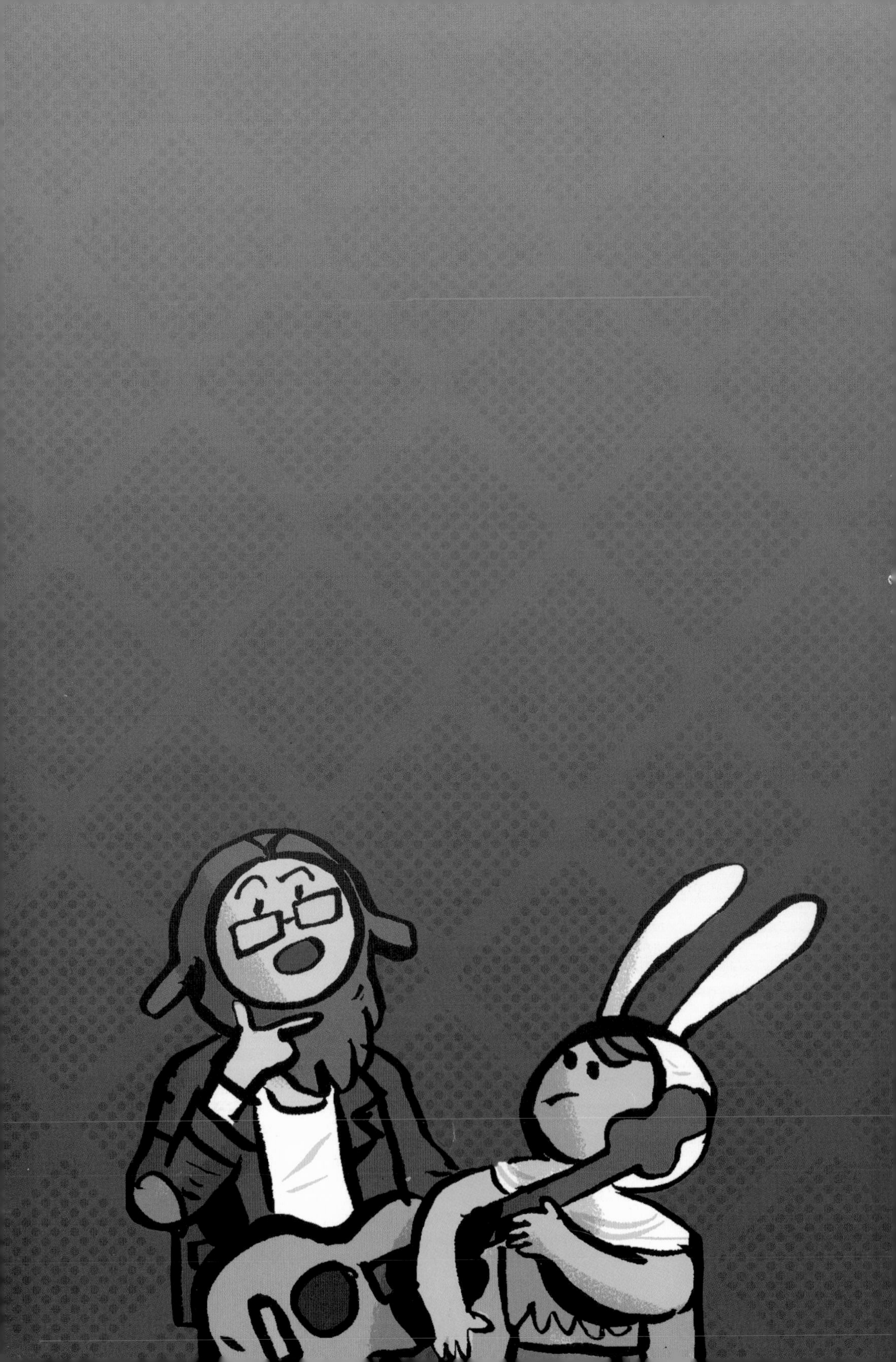

ADVENTURE TIME™

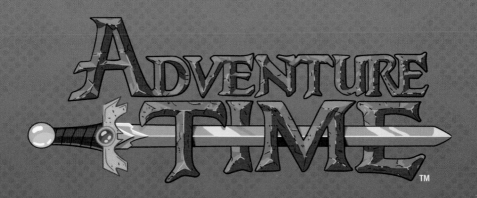

ISLANDS

ROSS RICHIE CEO & Founder • MATT GAGNON Editor-in-Chief • FILIP SABLIK President of Publishing & Marketing • STEPHEN CHRISTY President of Development • LANCE KREITER VP of Licensing & Merchandising • PHIL BARBARO VP of Finance • BRYCE CARLSON Managing Editor • MEL CAYLO Marketing Manager • SCOTT NEWMAN Production Design Manager • KATE HENNING Operations Manager • SIERRA HAHN Senior Editor • DAFNA PLEBAN Editor, Talent Development • SHANNON WATTERS Editor • ERIC HARBURN Editor • WHITNEY LEOPARD Associate Editor • JASMINE AMIRI Associate Editor • CHRIS ROSA Associate Editor • ALEX GALER Associate Editor • CAMERON CHITTOCK Associate Editor • MATTHEW LEVINE Assistant Editor • KELSEY DIETERICH Production Designer • JILLIAN CRAB Production Designer • MICHELLE ANKLEY Production Designer • GRACE PARK Production Design Assistant • AARON FERRARA Operations Coordinator • ELIZABETH LOUGHRIDGE Accounting Coordinator • STEPHANIE HOCUTT Social Media Coordinator • JOSÉ MEZA Sales Assistant • JAMES ARRIOLA Mailroom Assistant • HOLLY AITCHISON Operations Assistant • SAM KUSEK Direct Market Representative • AMBER PARKER Administrative Assistant

ADVENTURE TIME: ISLANDS, November 2016. Published by KaBOOM!, a division of Boom Entertainment, Inc. ADVENTURE TIME, CARTOON NETWORK, the logos, and all related characters and elements are trademarks of and © Cartoon Network. (S16) All rights reserved. KaBOOM!™ and the KaBOOM! logo are trademarks of Boom Entertainment, Inc., registered in various countries and categories. All characters, events, and institutions depicted herein are fictional. Any similarity between any of the names, characters, persons, events, and/or institutions in this publication to actual names, characters, and persons, whether living or dead, events, and/or institutions is unintended and purely coincidental. KaBOOM! does not read or accept unsolicited submissions of ideas, stories, or artwork.

For information regarding the CPSIA on this printed material, call: (203) 595-3636 and provide reference #RICH – 691481. A catalog record of this book is available from OCLC and from the BOOM! Studios website, www.boom-studios.com, on the Librarians Page.

BOOM! Studios, 5670 Wilshire Boulevard, Suite 450, Los Angeles, CA 90036-5679. Printed in USA. First Printing.
ISBN: 978-1-60886-972-5, eISBN: 978-1-61398-643-1

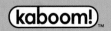

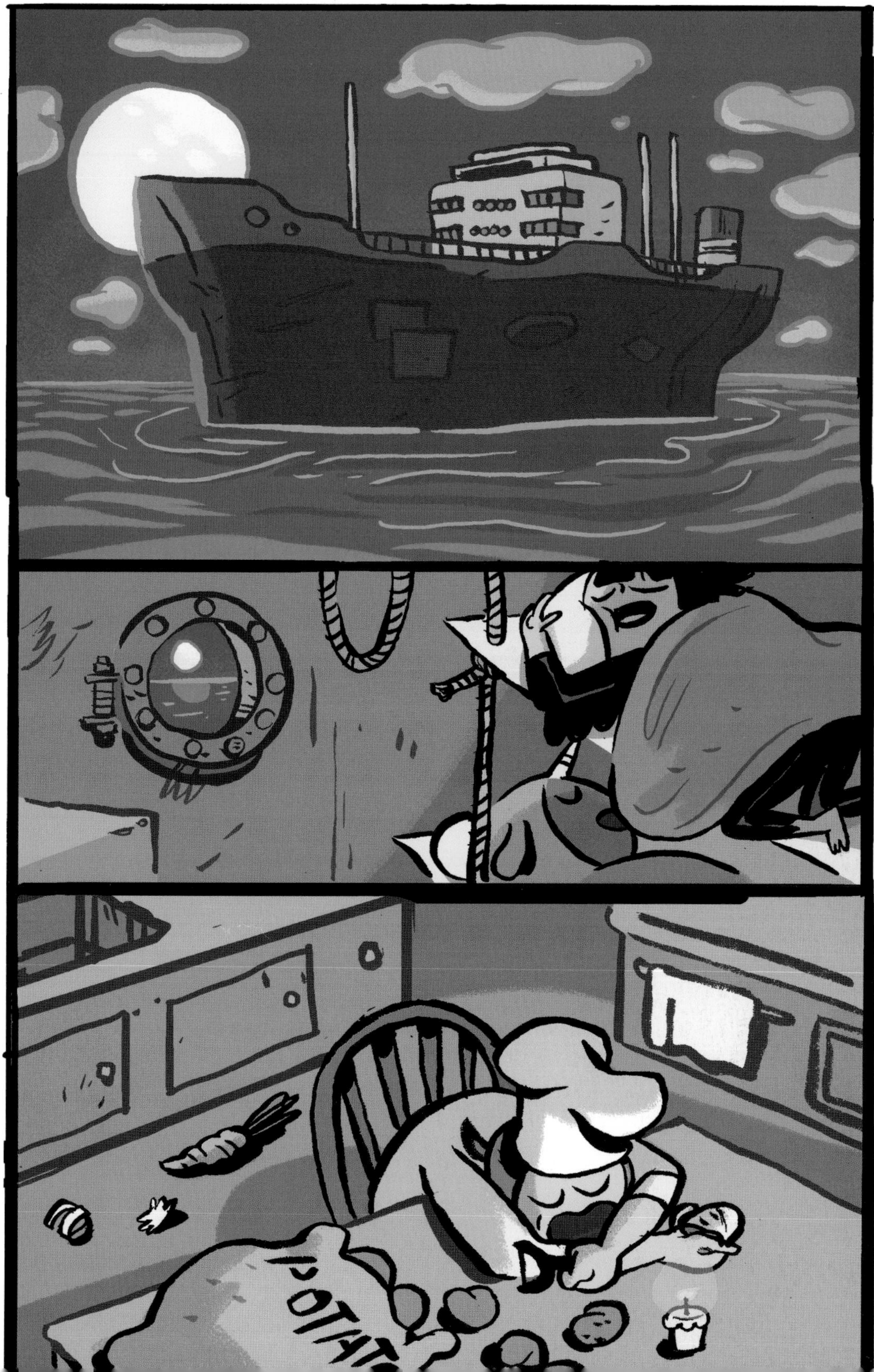
POTAT

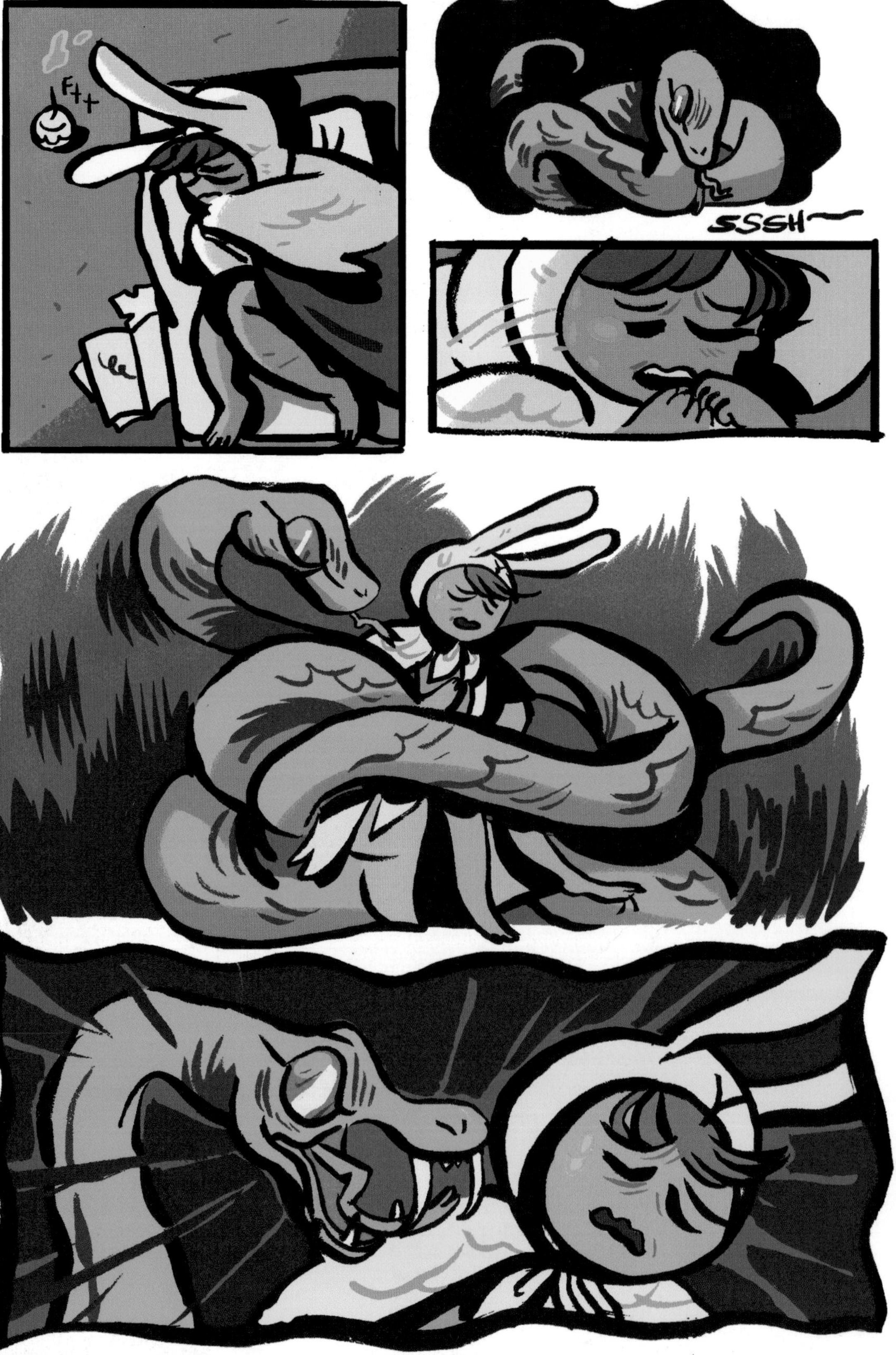

Ftt
SSSH~

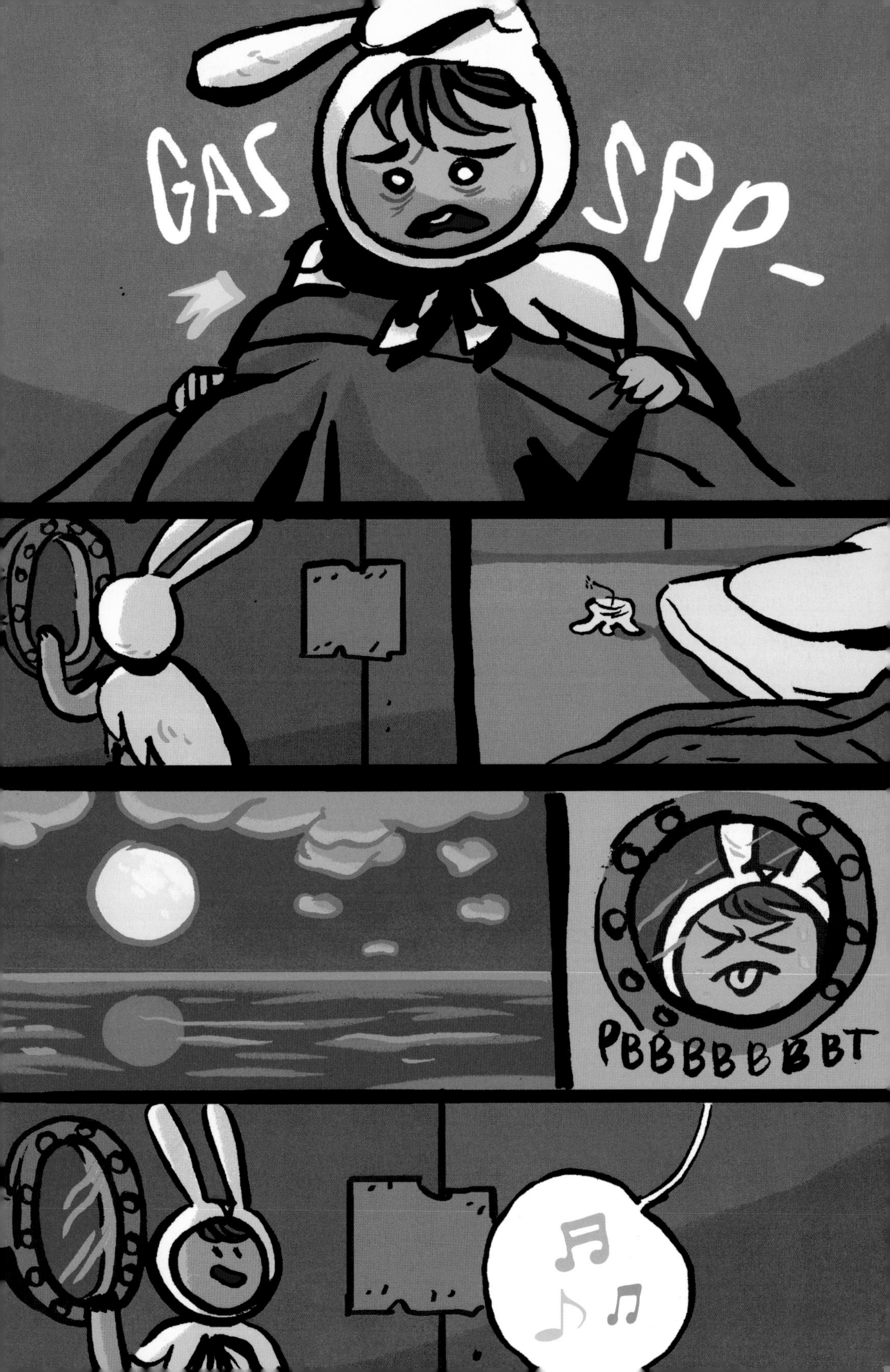
GASSPP-
PBBBBBBBT

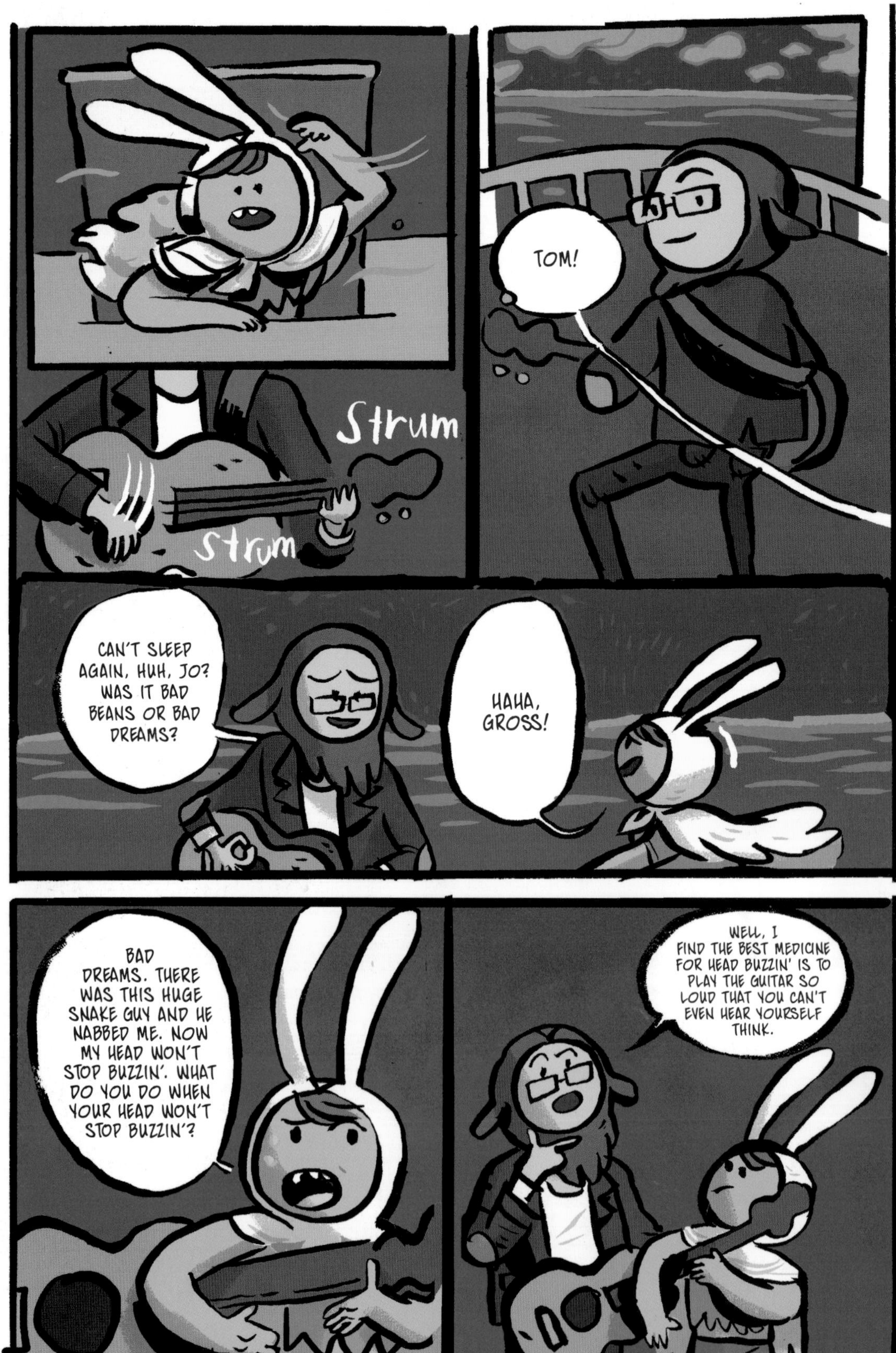
Strum
Strum
TOM!
CAN'T SLEEP AGAIN, HUH, JO? WAS IT BAD BEANS OR BAD DREAMS?
HAHA, GROSS!
BAD DREAMS. THERE WAS THIS HUGE SNAKE GUY AND HE NABBED ME. NOW MY HEAD WON'T STOP BUZZIN'. WHAT DO YOU DO WHEN YOUR HEAD WON'T STOP BUZZIN'?
WELL, I FIND THE BEST MEDICINE FOR HEAD BUZZIN' IS TO PLAY THE GUITAR SO LOUD THAT YOU CAN'T EVEN HEAR YOURSELF THINK.

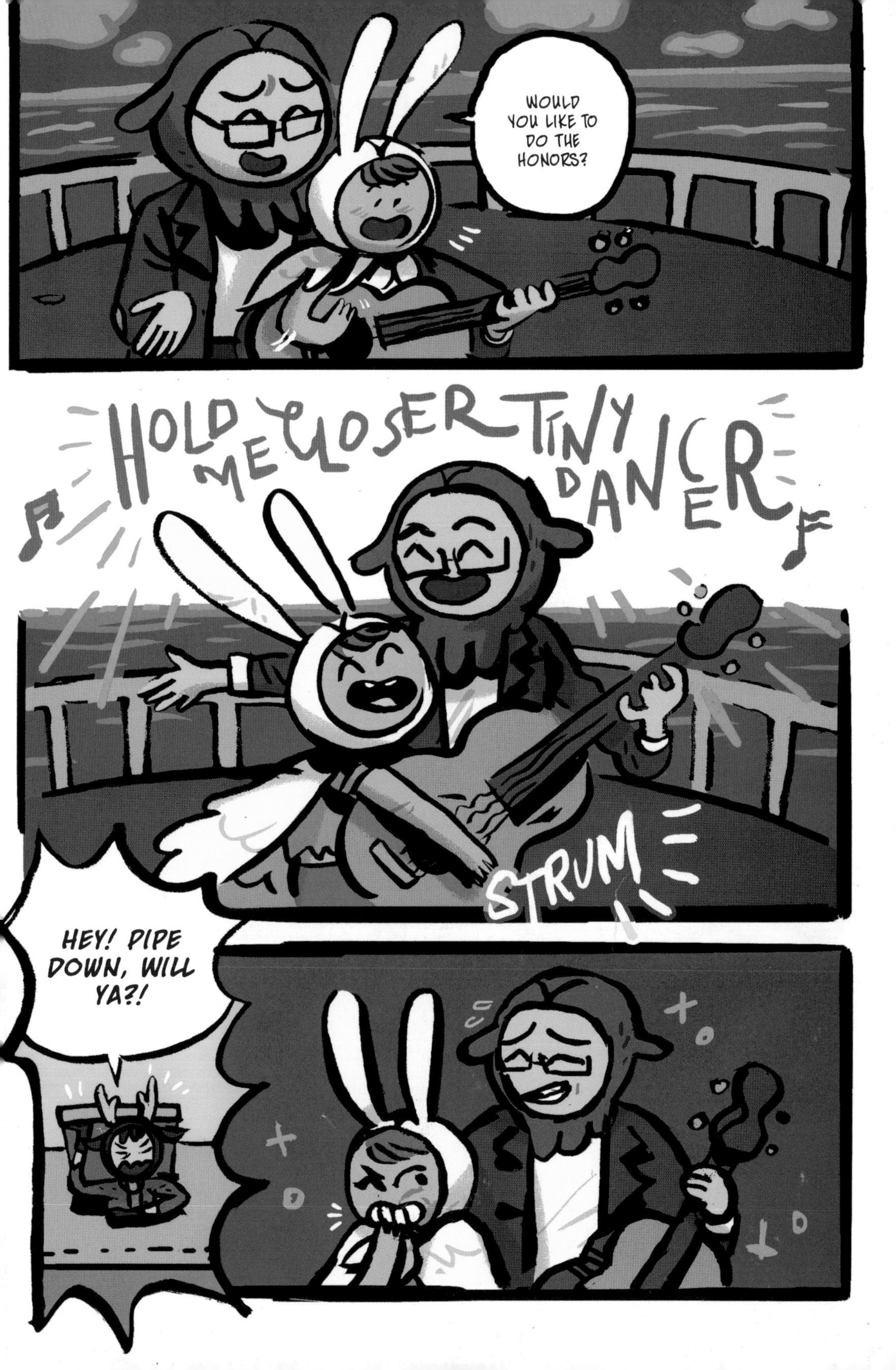
WOULD YOU LIKE TO DO THE HONORS?
HOLD ME CLOSER TINY DANCER
STRUM
HEY! PIPE DOWN, WILL YA?!

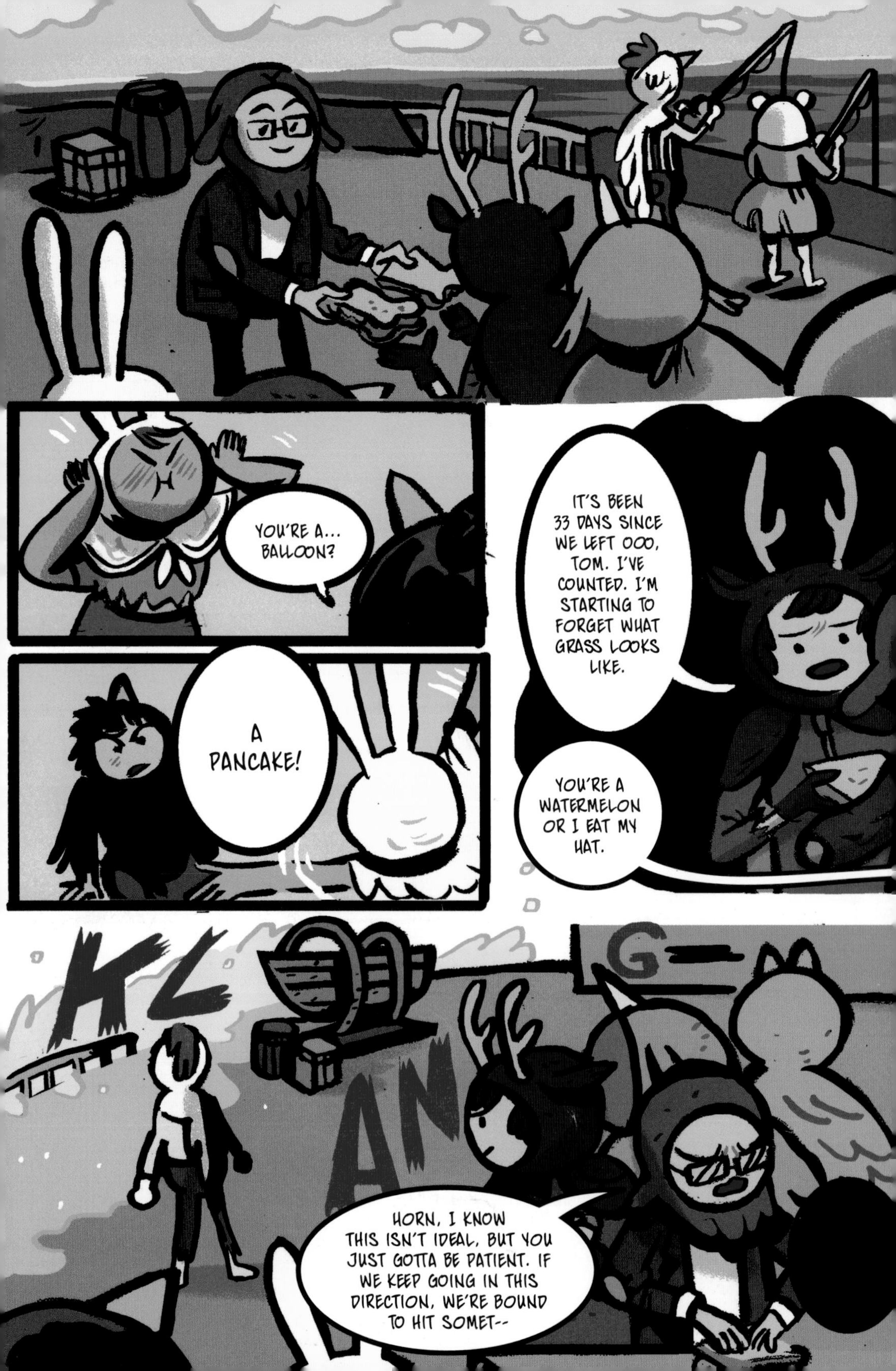

YOU'RE A... BALLOON?
A PANCAKE!
IT'S BEEN 33 DAYS SINCE WE LEFT OOO, TOM. I'VE COUNTED. I'M STARTING TO FORGET WHAT GRASS LOOKS LIKE.
YOU'RE A WATERMELON OR I EAT MY HAT.
KLANG
HORN, I KNOW THIS ISN'T IDEAL, BUT YOU JUST GOTTA BE PATIENT. IF WE KEEP GOING IN THIS DIRECTION, WE'RE BOUND TO HIT SOMET--

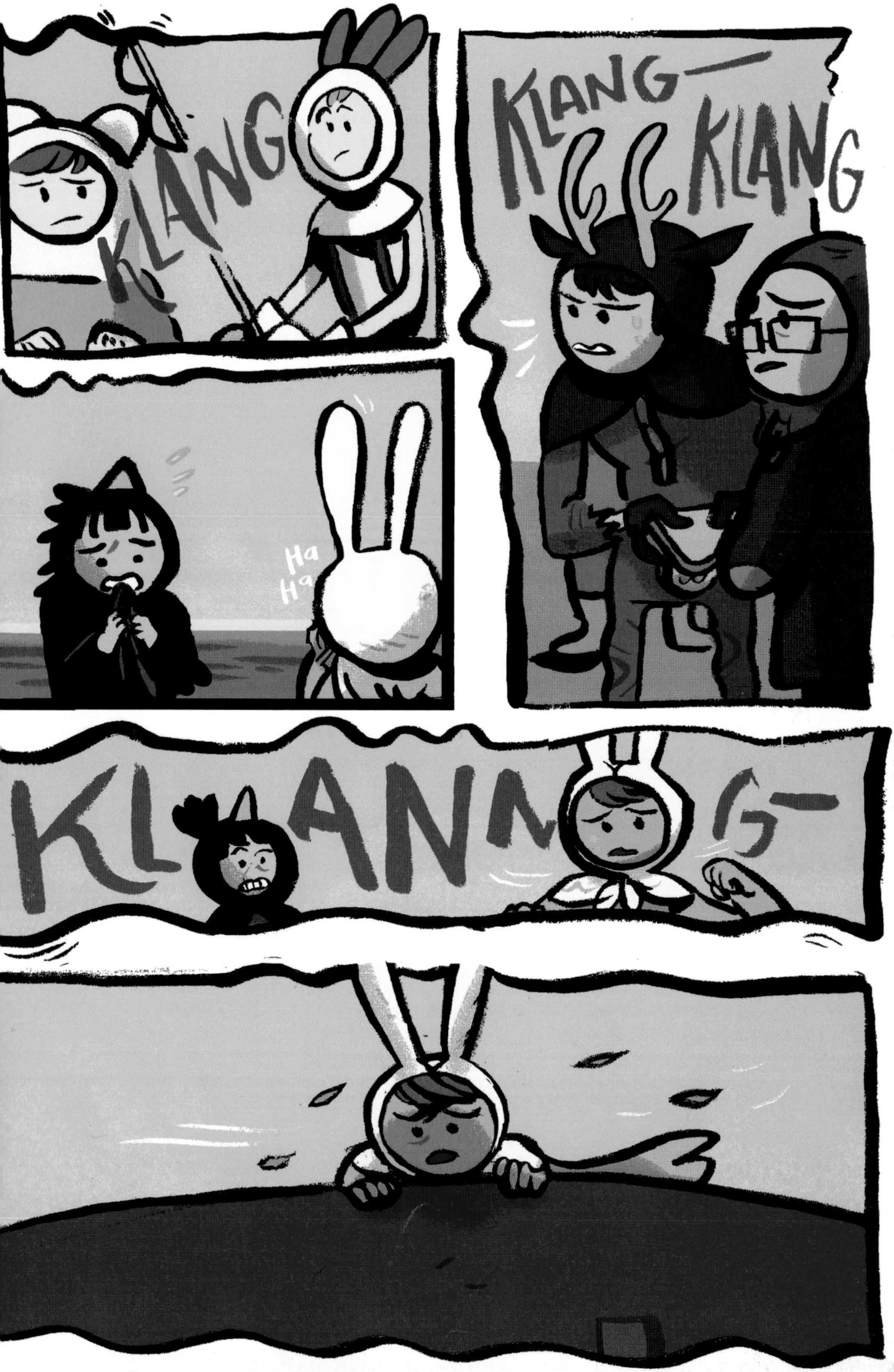
KLANG
KLANG—
KLANG
Ha
Ha
KLANNG—

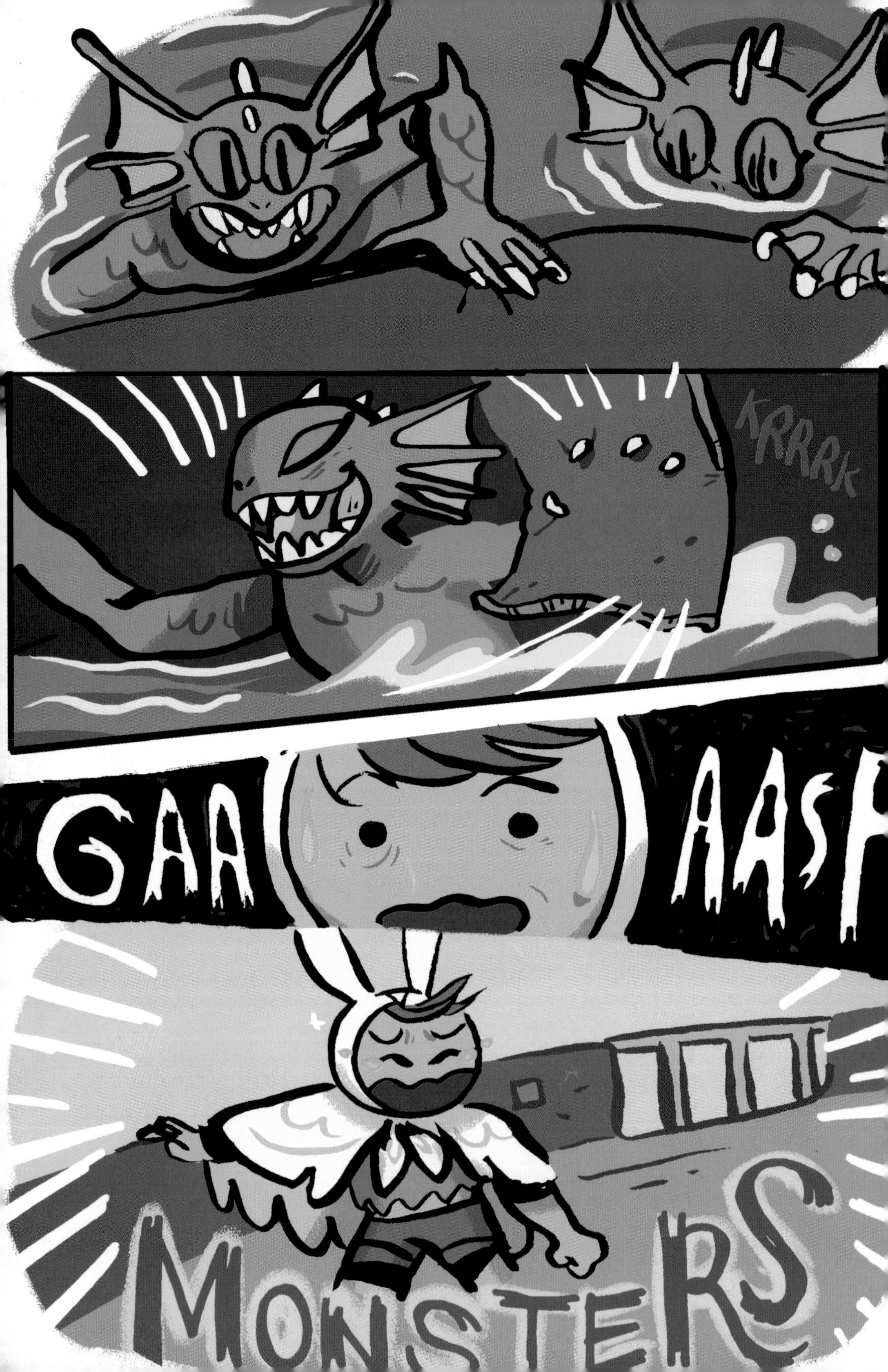
KRRRK
GAA
AASP
MONSTERS

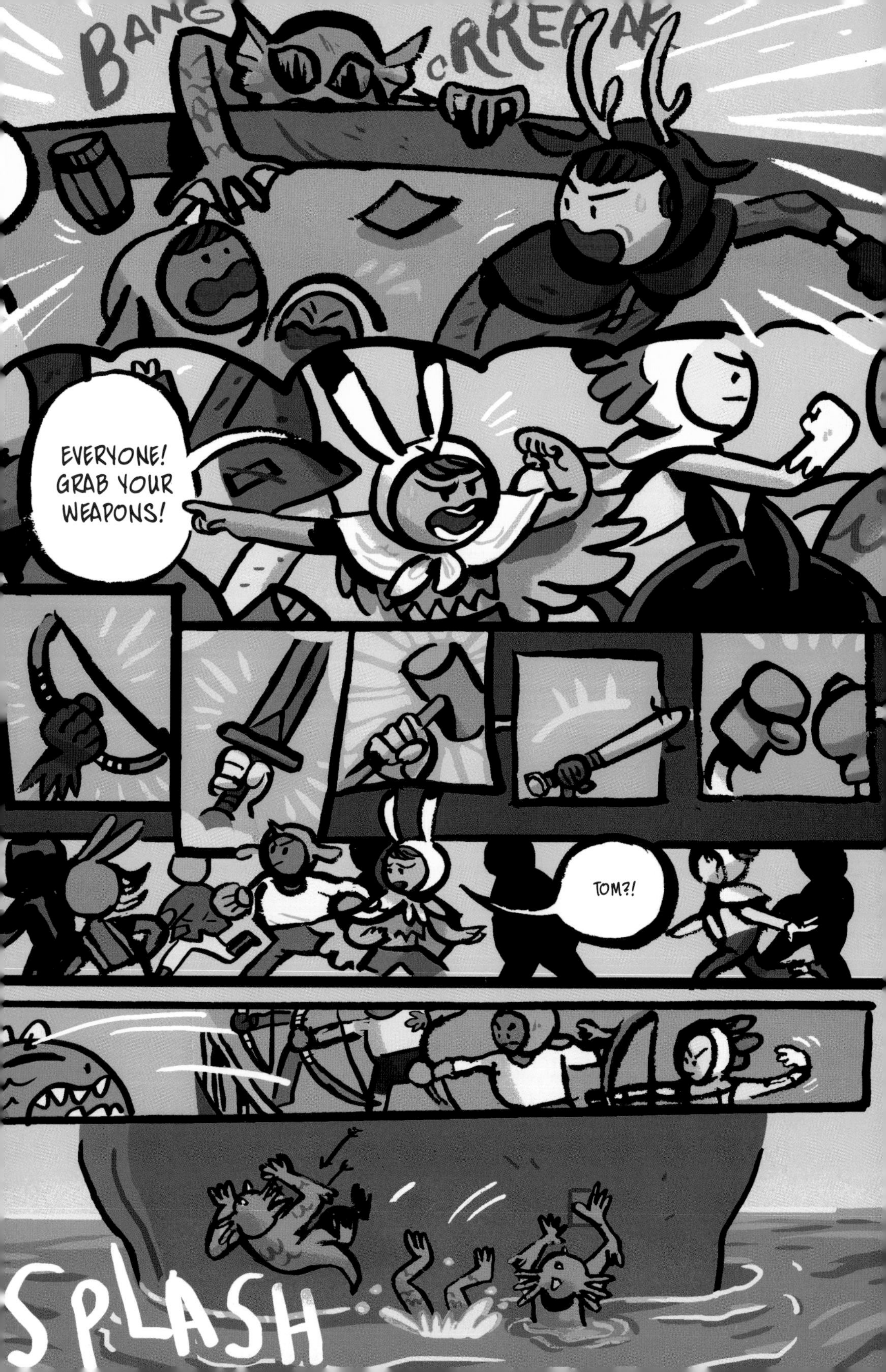
BANG
CRREAAK
EVERYONE! GRAB YOUR WEAPONS!
TOM?!
SPLASH

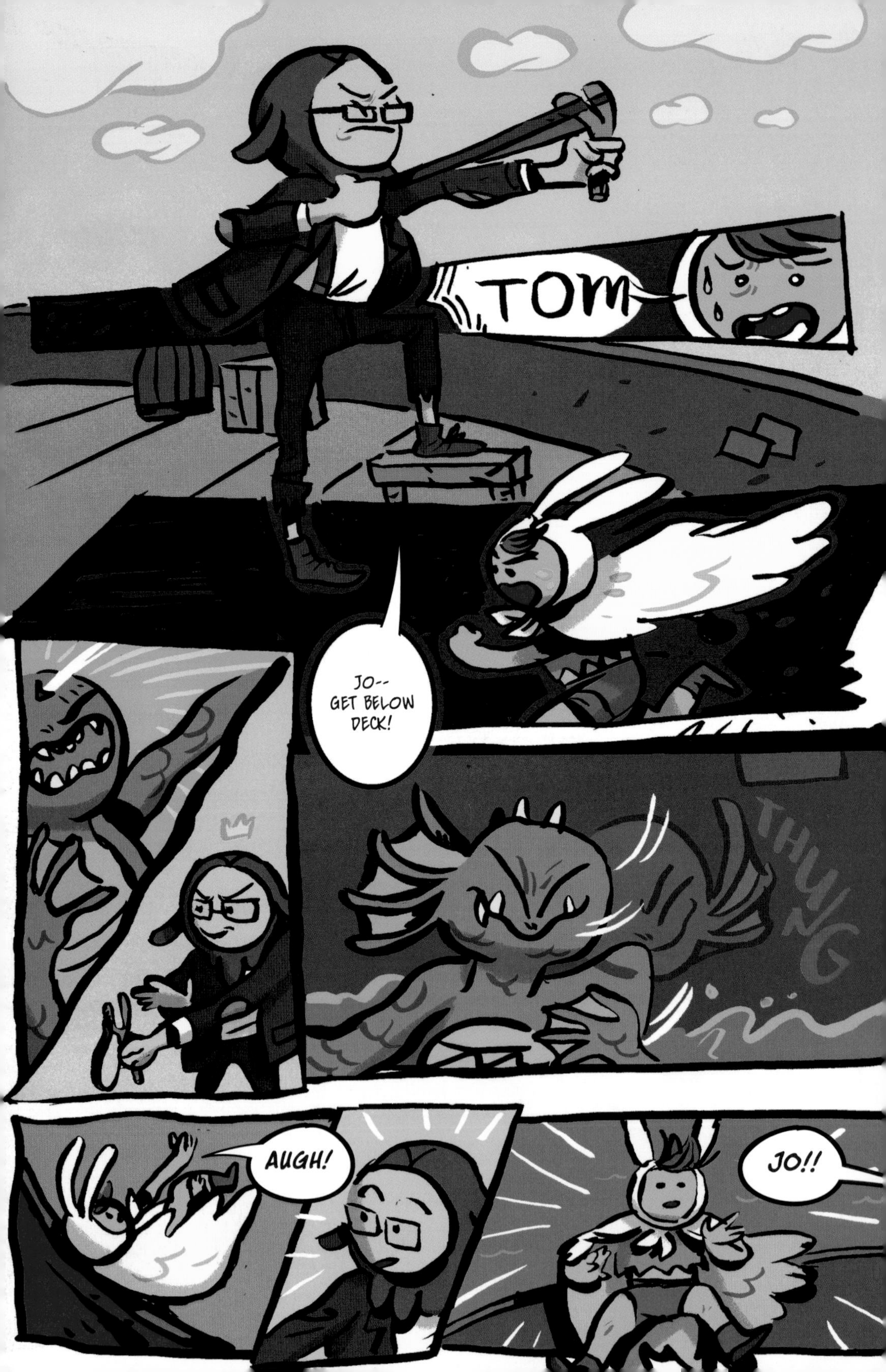
TOM
JO-- GET BELOW DECK!
THUNG
AUGH!
JO!!

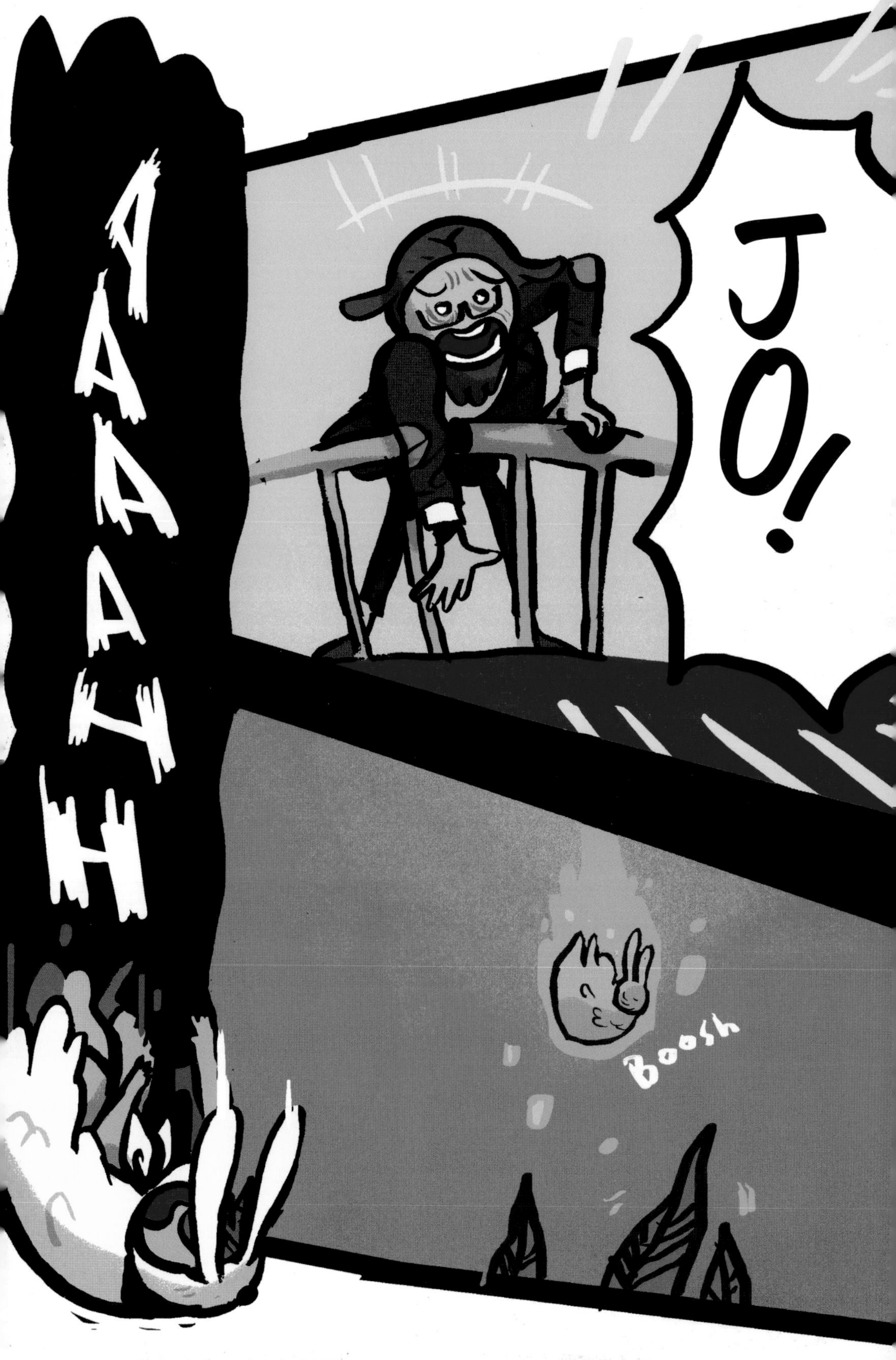
JO!
AAAAHH
Boosh

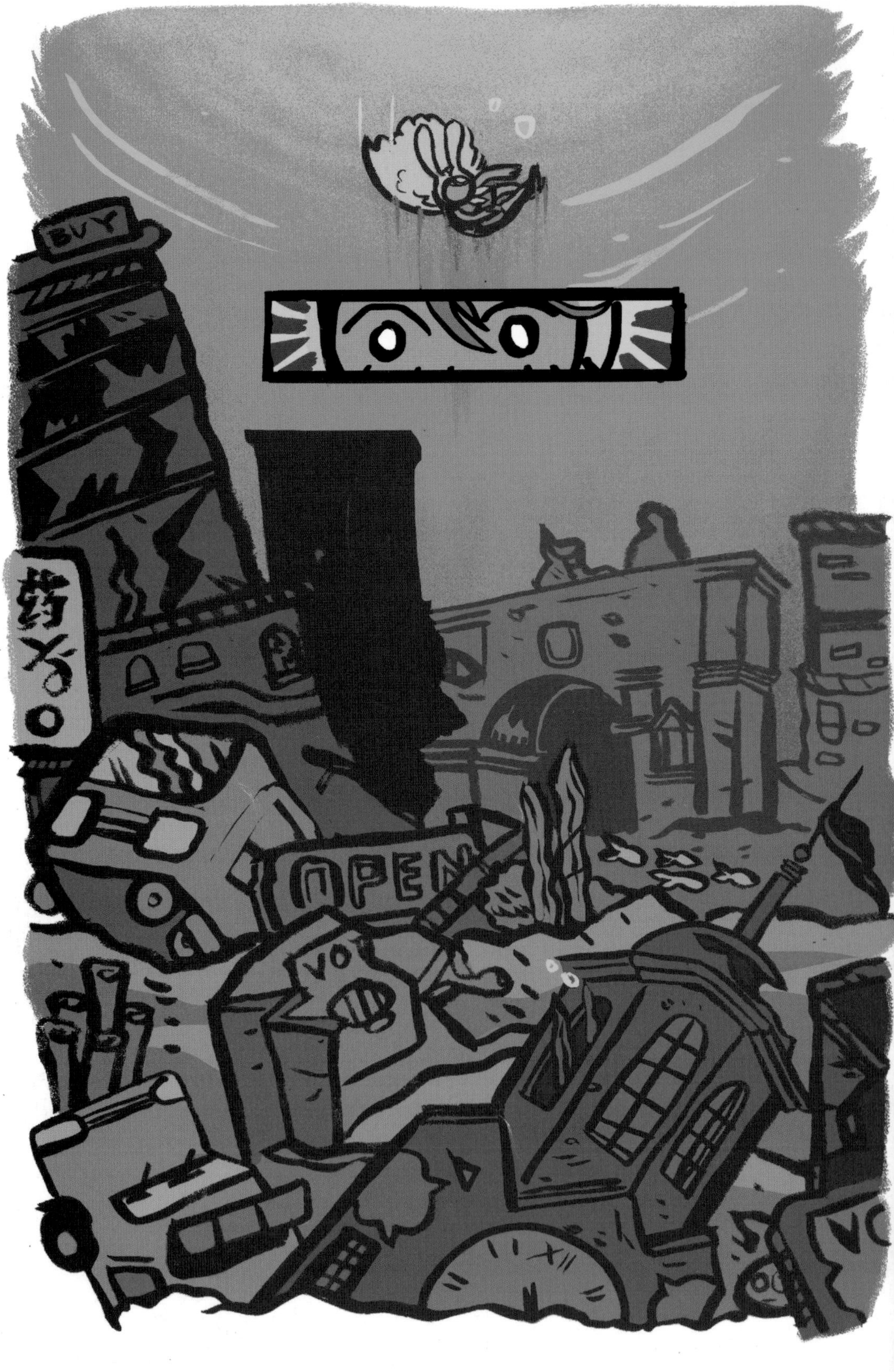
BUY
OPEN
VOT
VO

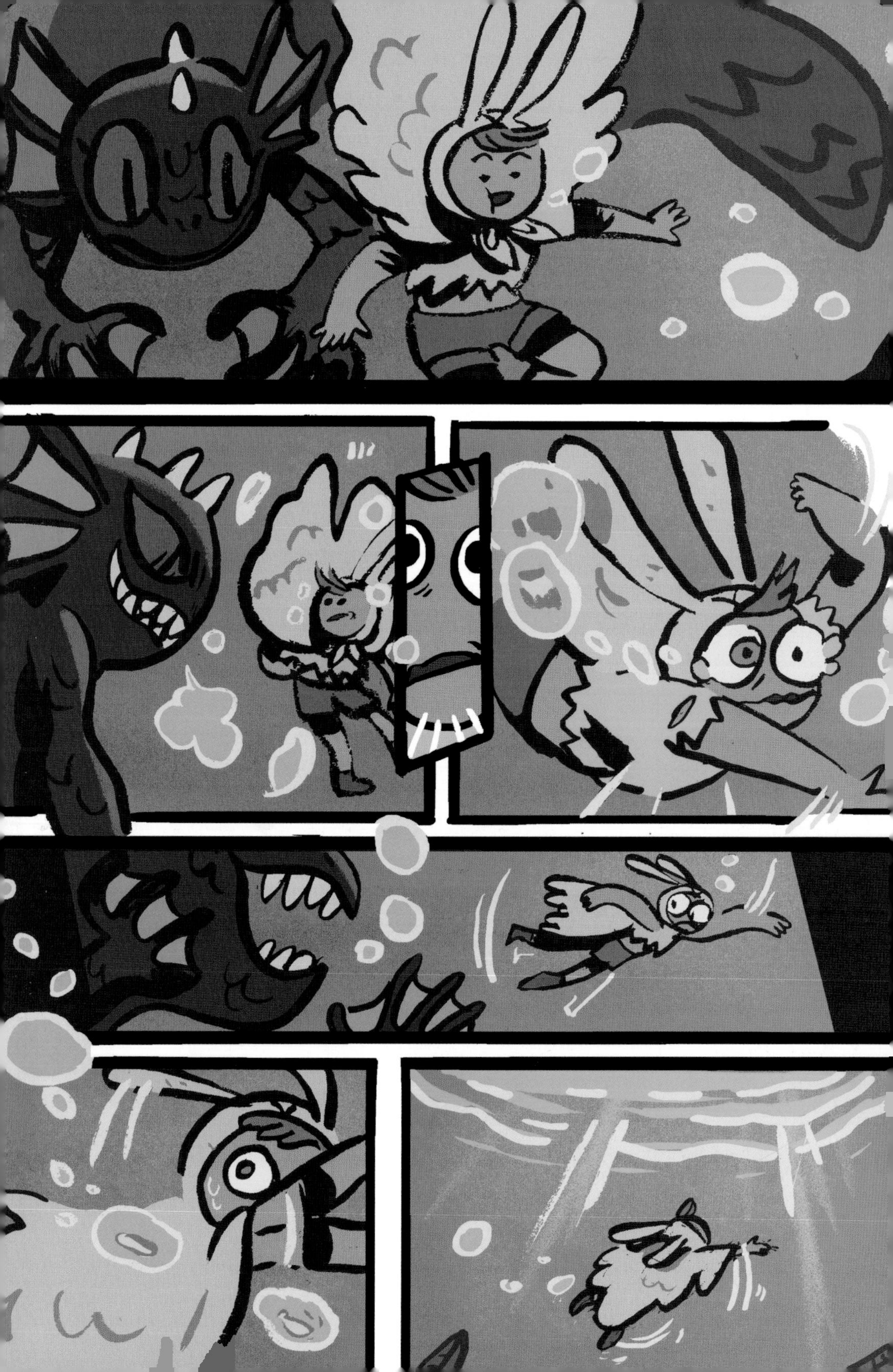

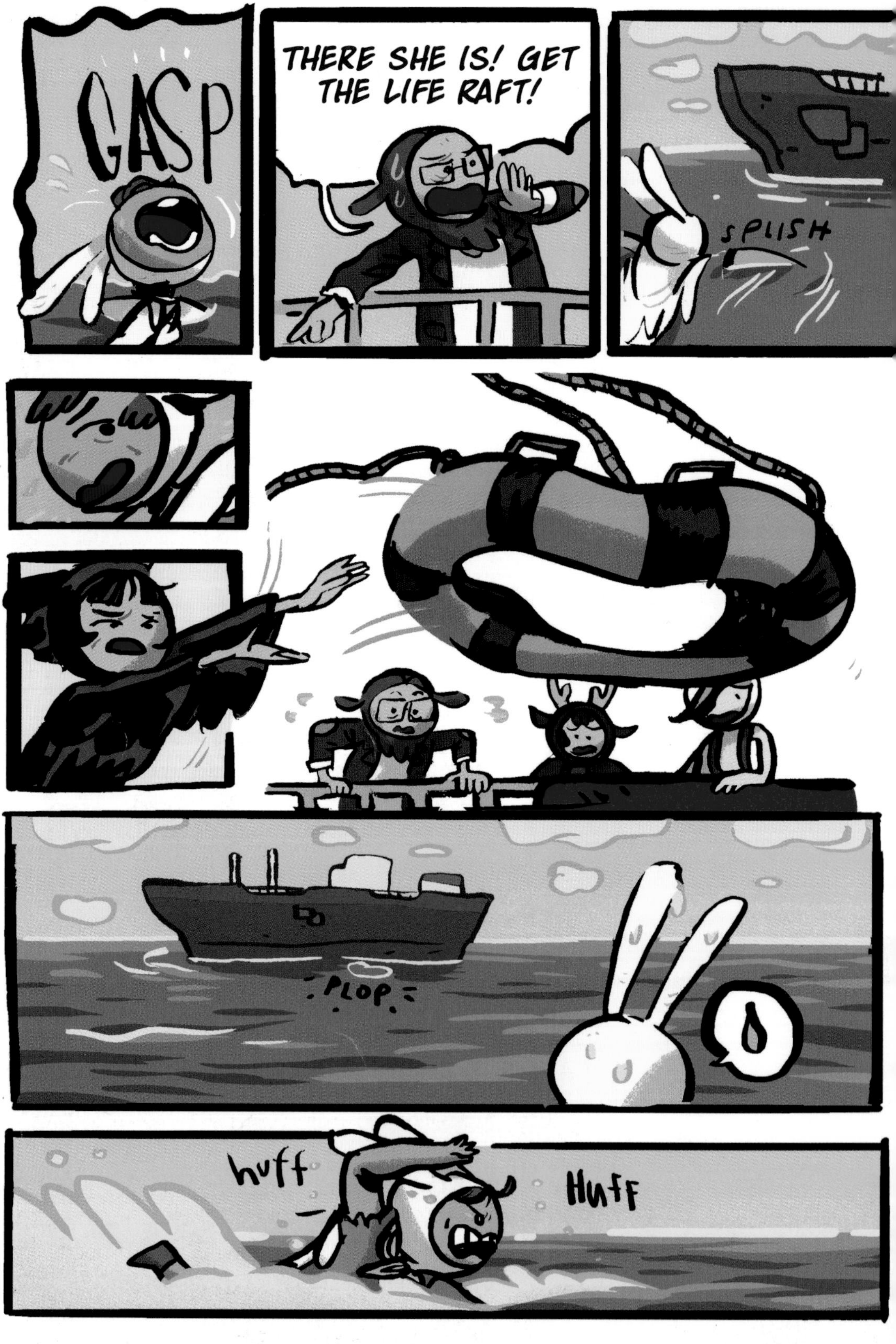
GASP
THERE SHE IS! GET THE LIFE RAFT!
SPLISH
PLOP
huff
Huff

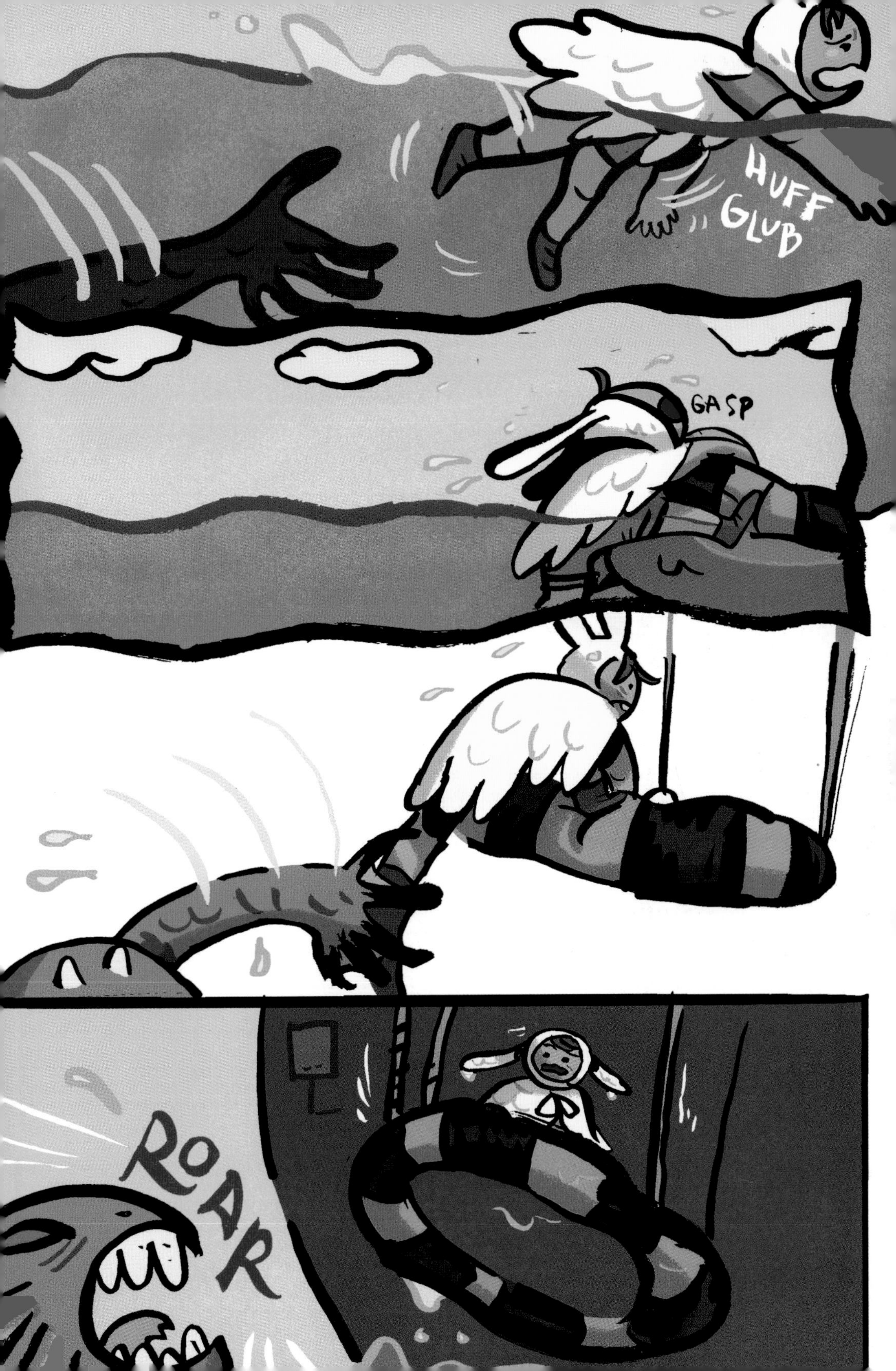
HUFF
GLUB
GASP
ROAR

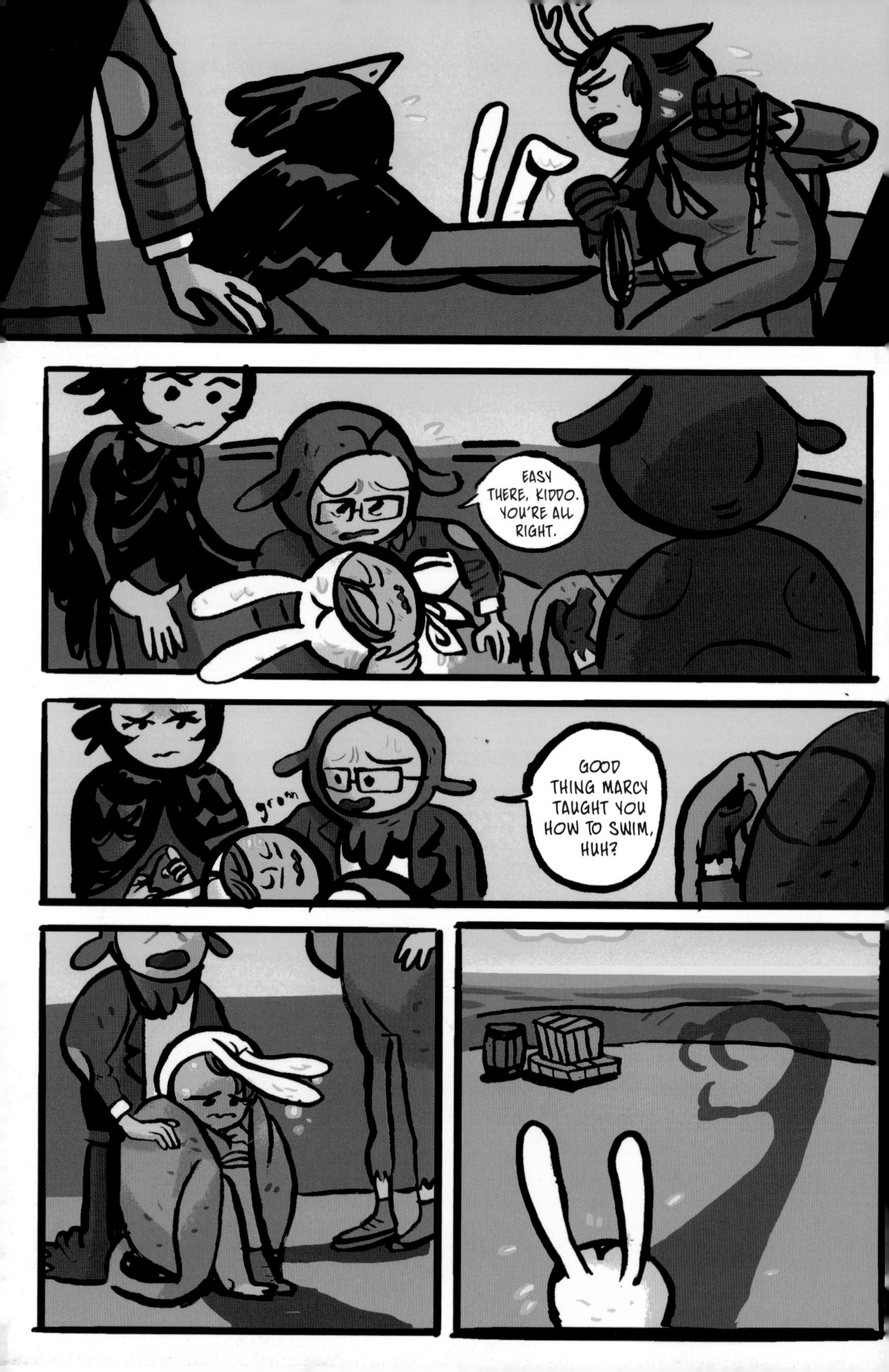
EASY THERE, KIDDO. YOU'RE ALL RIGHT.
groan
GOOD THING MARCY TAUGHT YOU HOW TO SWIM, HUH?

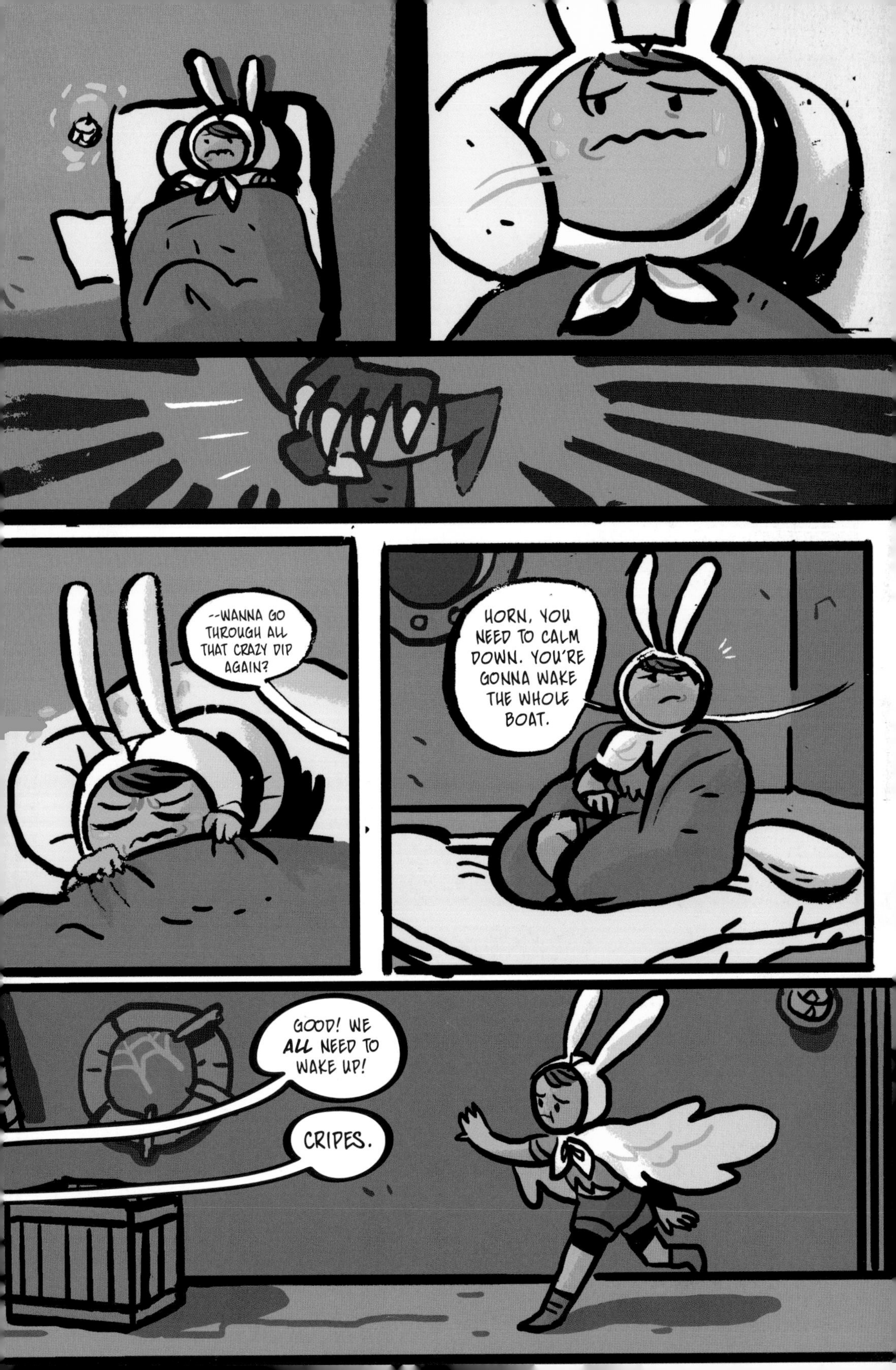
--WANNA GO THROUGH ALL THAT CRAZY DIP AGAIN?
HORN, YOU NEED TO CALM DOWN. YOU'RE GONNA WAKE THE WHOLE BOAT.
GOOD! WE ALL NEED TO WAKE UP!
CRIPES.

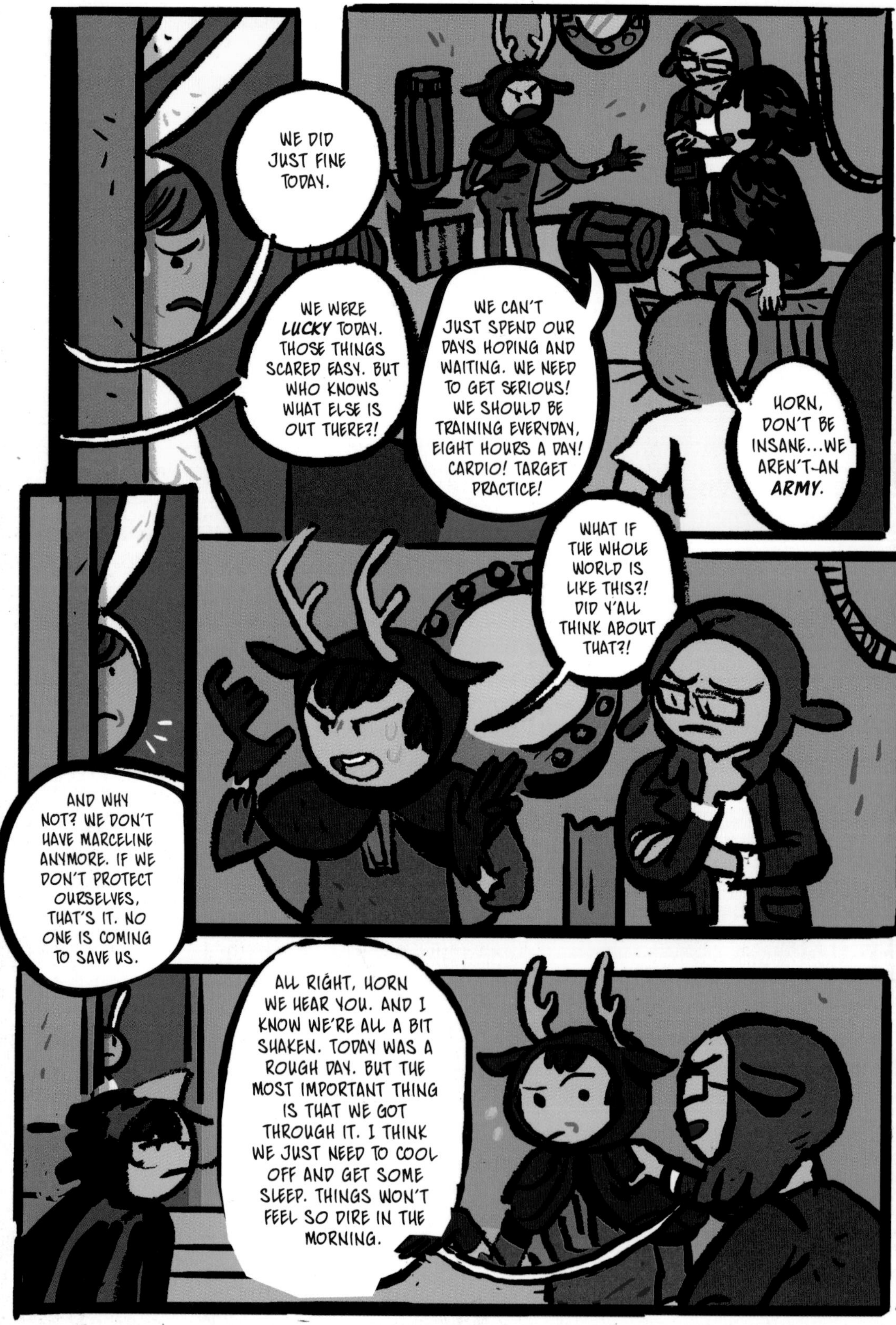
WE DID JUST FINE TODAY.
WE WERE LUCKY TODAY. THOSE THINGS SCARED EASY. BUT WHO KNOWS WHAT ELSE IS OUT THERE?!
WE CAN'T JUST SPEND OUR DAYS HOPING AND WAITING. WE NEED TO GET SERIOUS! WE SHOULD BE TRAINING EVERYDAY, EIGHT HOURS A DAY! CARDIO! TARGET PRACTICE!
HORN, DON'T BE INSANE...WE AREN'T AN ARMY.
AND WHY NOT? WE DON'T HAVE MARCELINE ANYMORE. IF WE DON'T PROTECT OURSELVES, THAT'S IT. NO ONE IS COMING TO SAVE US.
WHAT IF THE WHOLE WORLD IS LIKE THIS?! DID Y'ALL THINK ABOUT THAT?!
ALL RIGHT, HORN WE HEAR YOU. AND I KNOW WE'RE ALL A BIT SHAKEN. TODAY WAS A ROUGH DAY. BUT THE MOST IMPORTANT THING IS THAT WE GOT THROUGH IT. I THINK WE JUST NEED TO COOL OFF AND GET SOME SLEEP. THINGS WON'T FEEL SO DIRE IN THE MORNING.

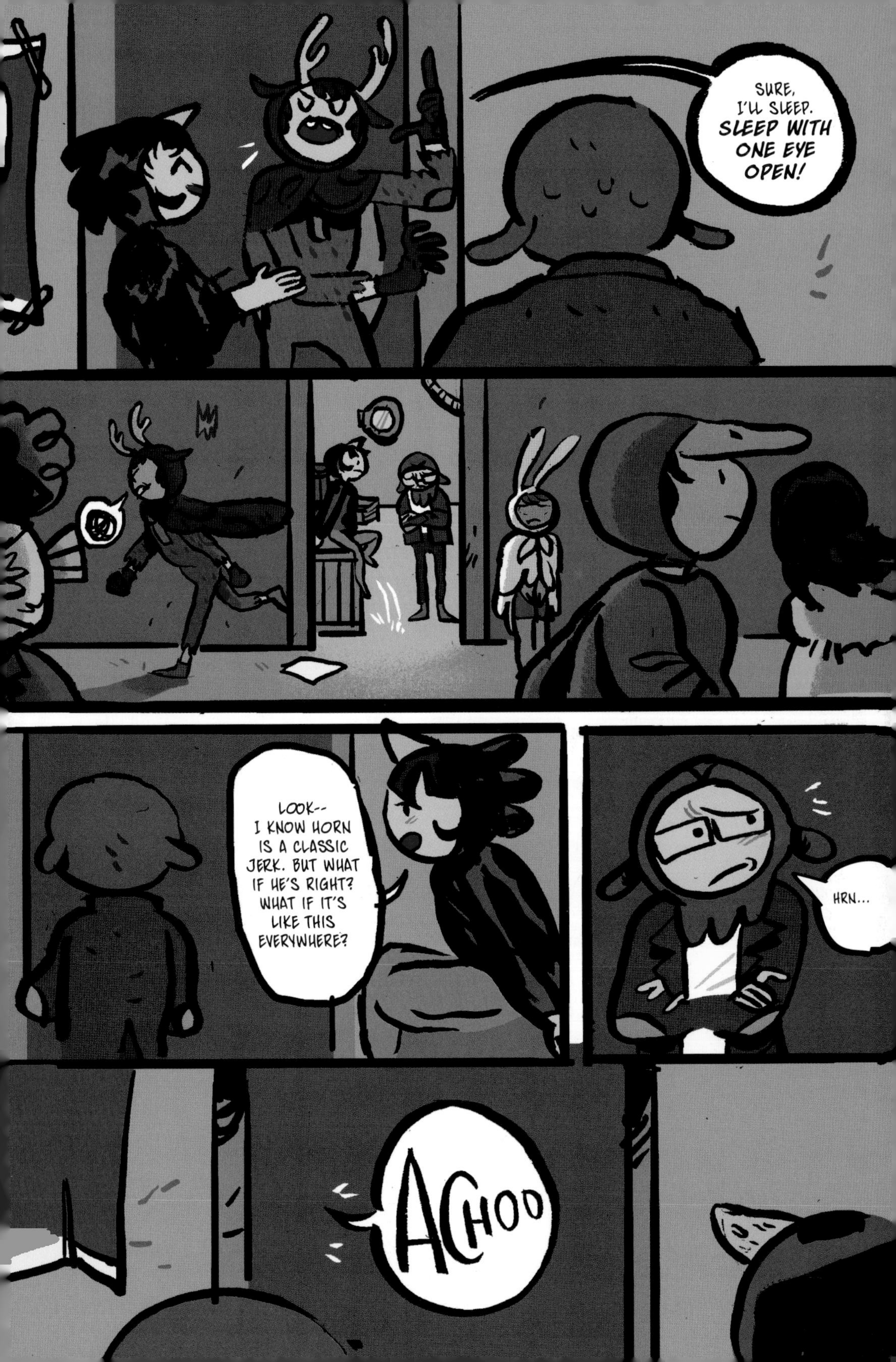
SURE, I'LL SLEEP. SLEEP WITH ONE EYE OPEN!
LOOK-- I KNOW HORN IS A CLASSIC JERK. BUT WHAT IF HE'S RIGHT? WHAT IF IT'S LIKE THIS EVERYWHERE?
HRN...
ACHOO

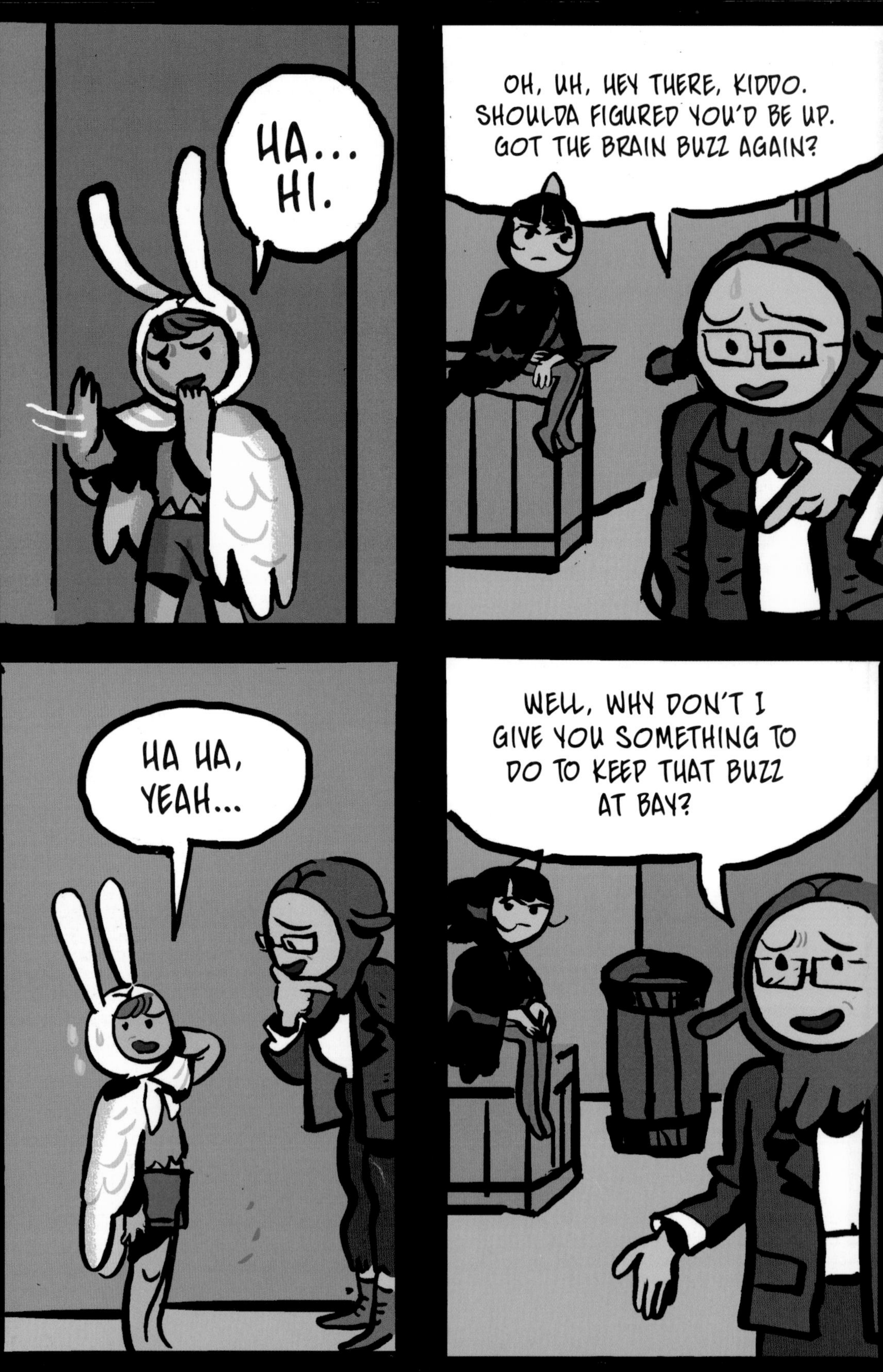
HA... HI.
OH, UH, HEY THERE, KIDDO. SHOULDA FIGURED YOU'D BE UP. GOT THE BRAIN BUZZ AGAIN?
HA HA, YEAH...
WELL, WHY DON'T I GIVE YOU SOMETHING TO DO TO KEEP THAT BUZZ AT BAY?

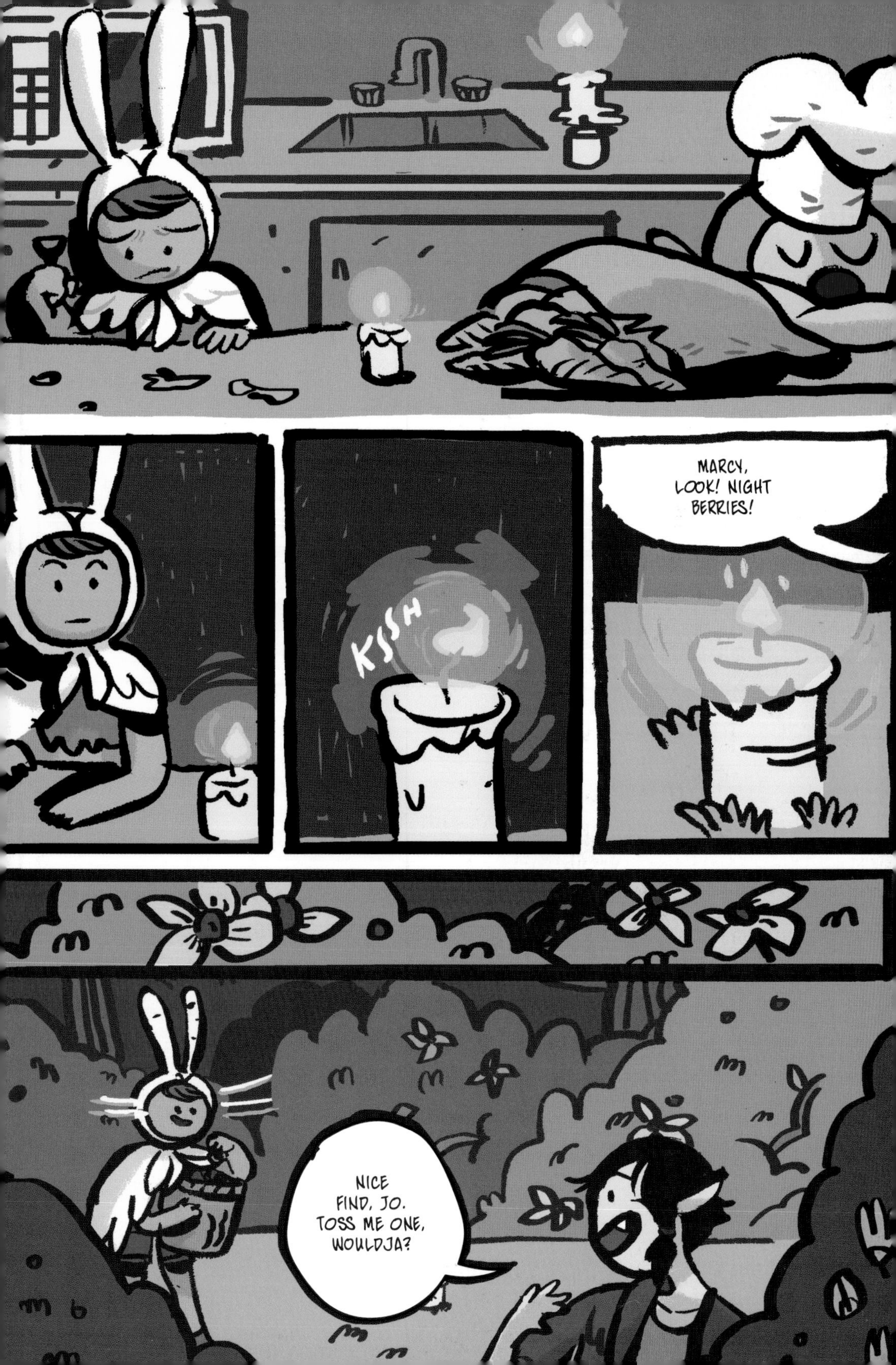
KSSH
MARCY, LOOK! NIGHT BERRIES!
NICE FIND, JO. TOSS ME ONE, WOULDJA?

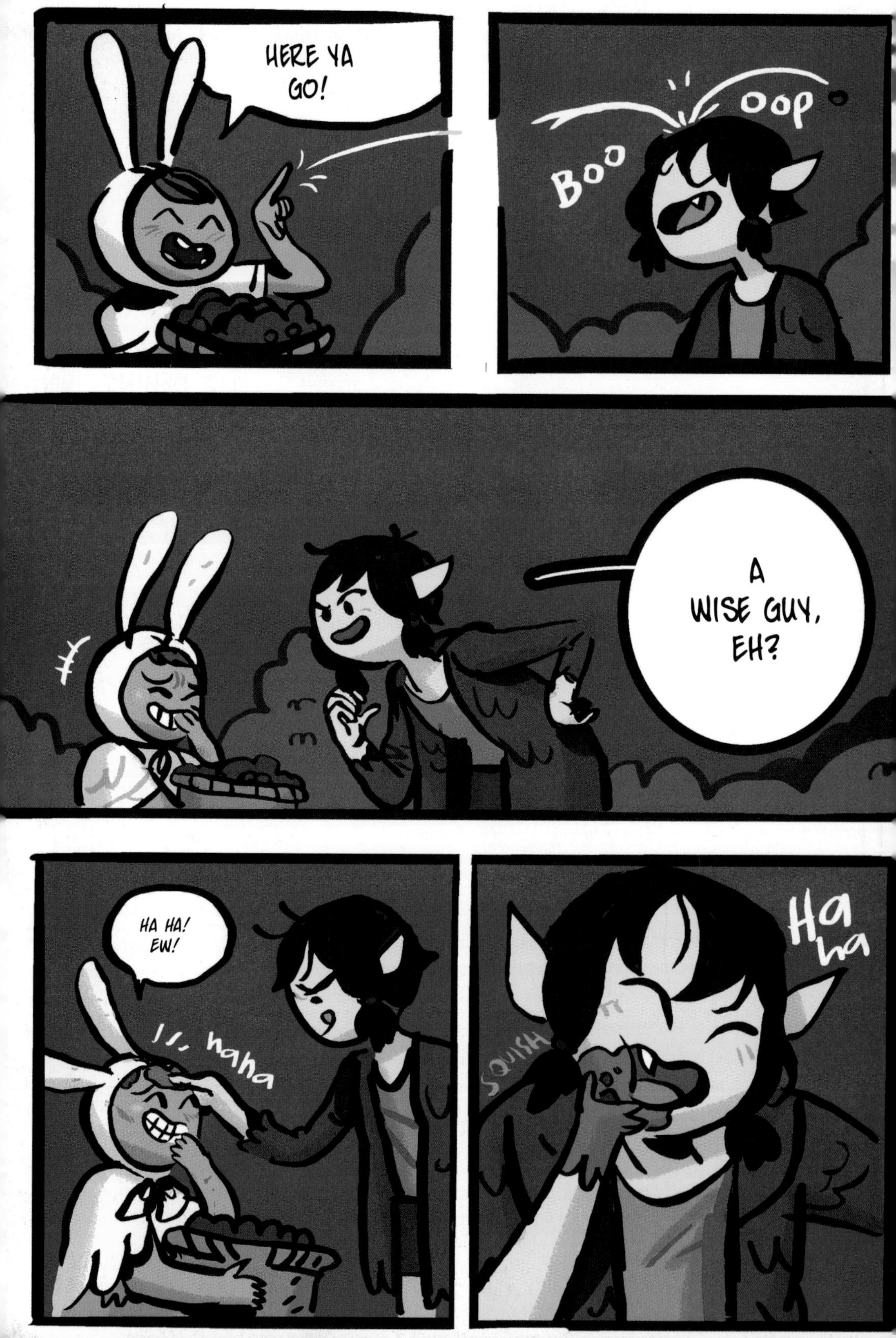
HERE YA GO!
BOO
OOP
A WISE GUY, EH?
HA HA! EW!
haha
SQUISH
Ha ha

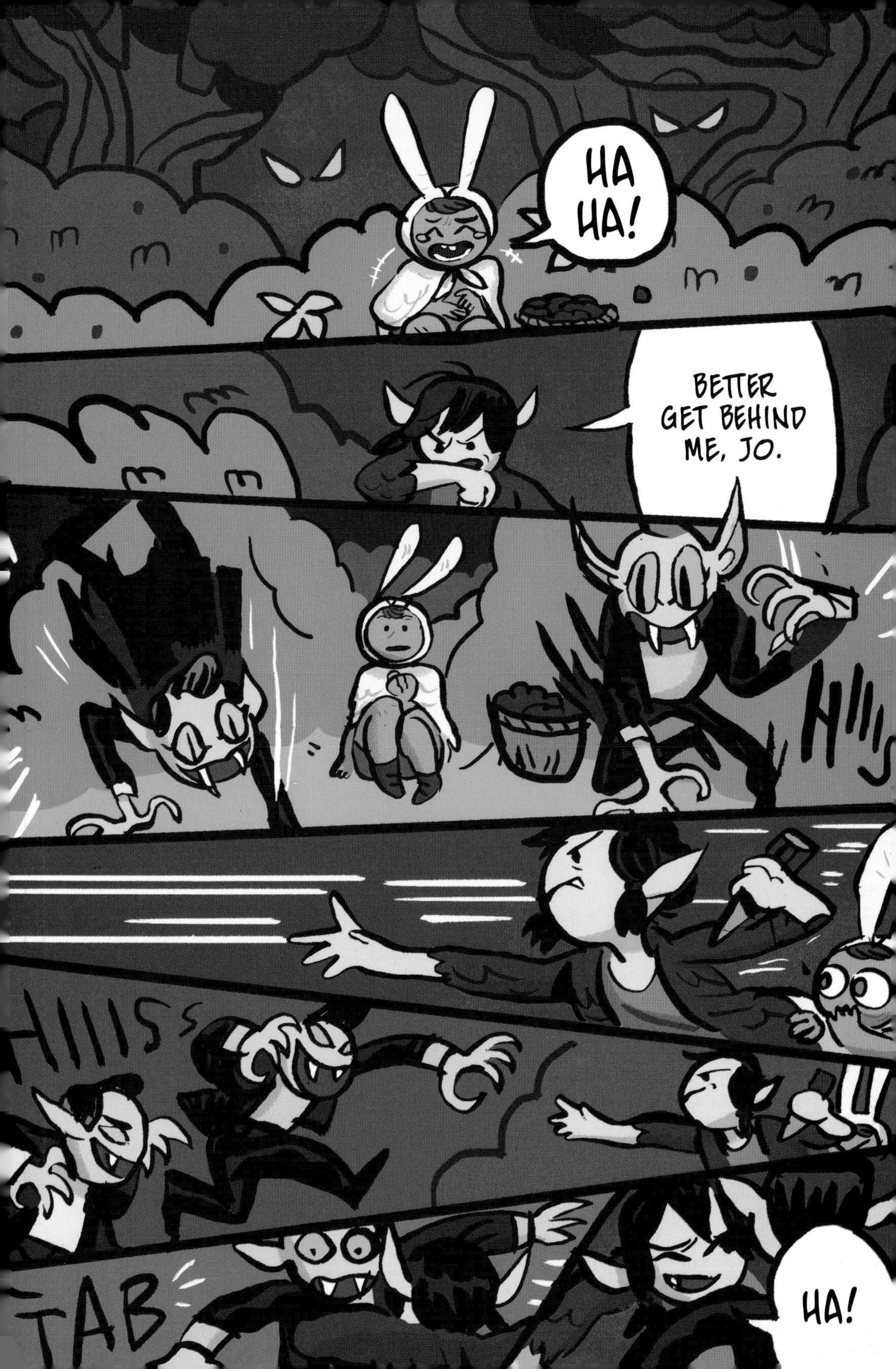
HA HA!
BETTER GET BEHIND ME, JO.
HIIIS
HIIISS
TAB
HA!

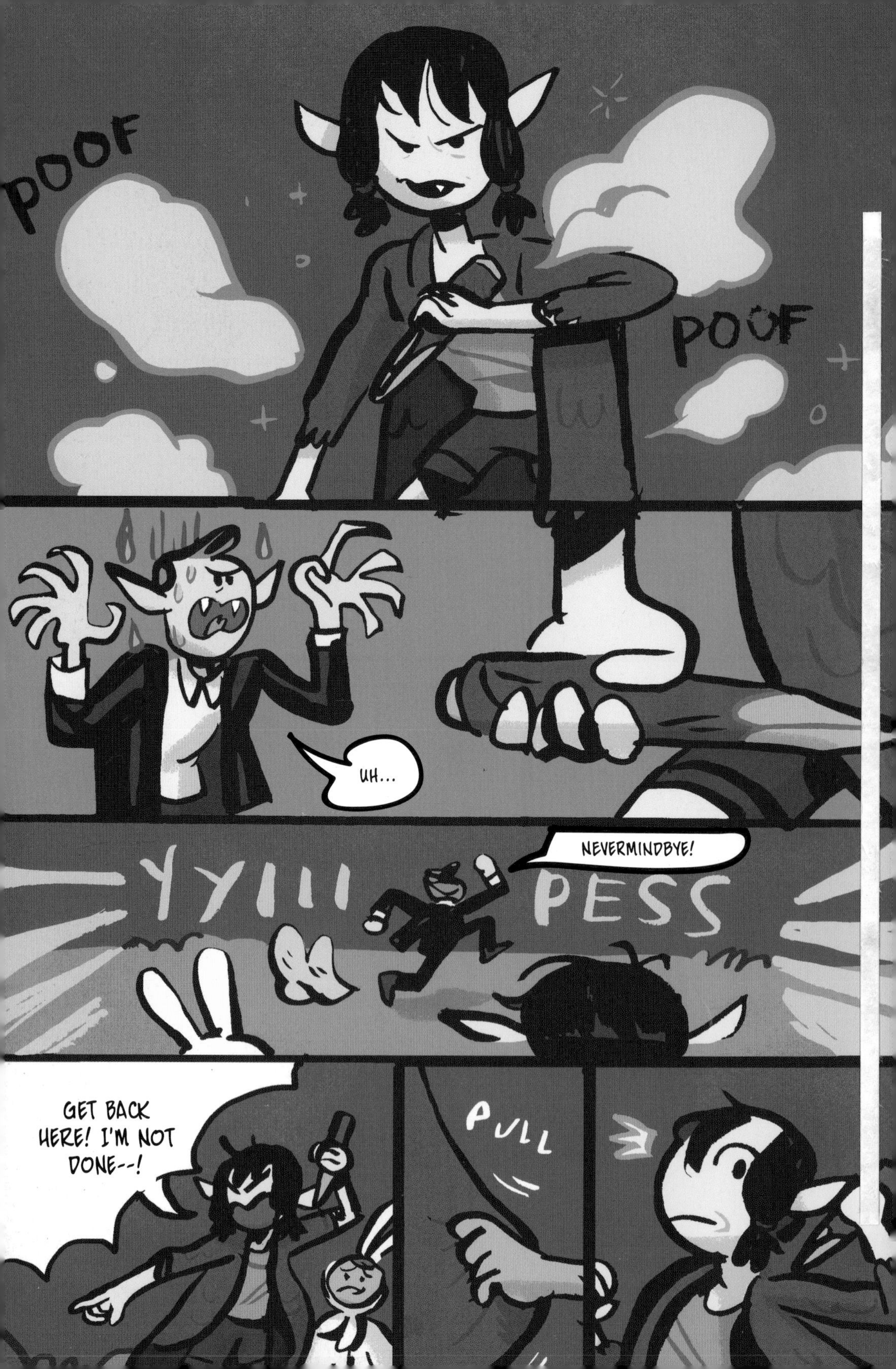
POOF
POOF
UH...
YYIII PESS
NEVERMINDBYE!
GET BACK HERE! I'M NOT DONE--!
PULL

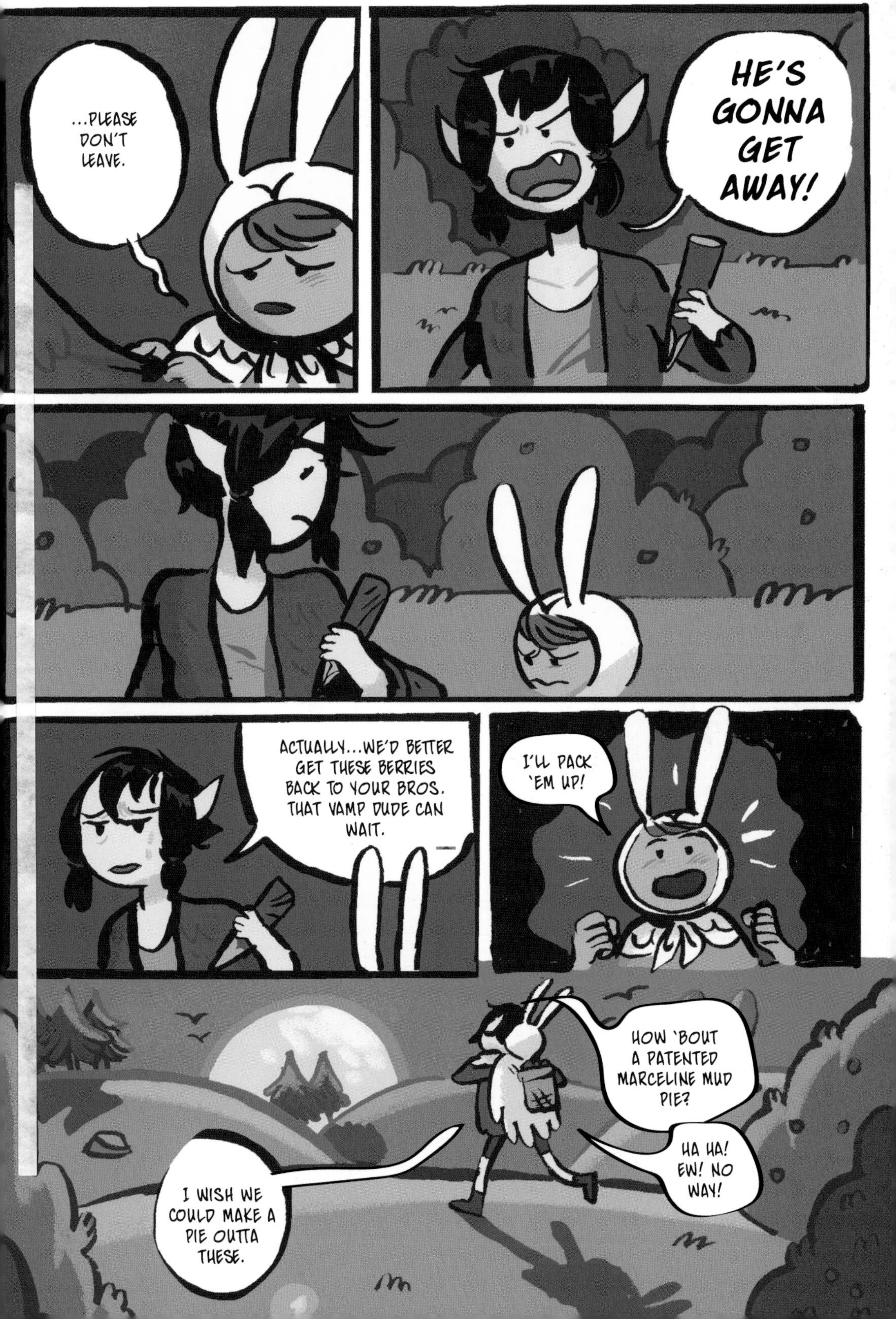
...PLEASE DON'T LEAVE.
HE'S GONNA GET AWAY!
ACTUALLY...WE'D BETTER GET THESE BERRIES BACK TO YOUR BROS. THAT VAMP DUDE CAN WAIT.
I'LL PACK 'EM UP!
I WISH WE COULD MAKE A PIE OUTTA THESE.
HOW 'BOUT A PATENTED MARCELINE MUD PIE?
HA HA! EW! NO WAY!

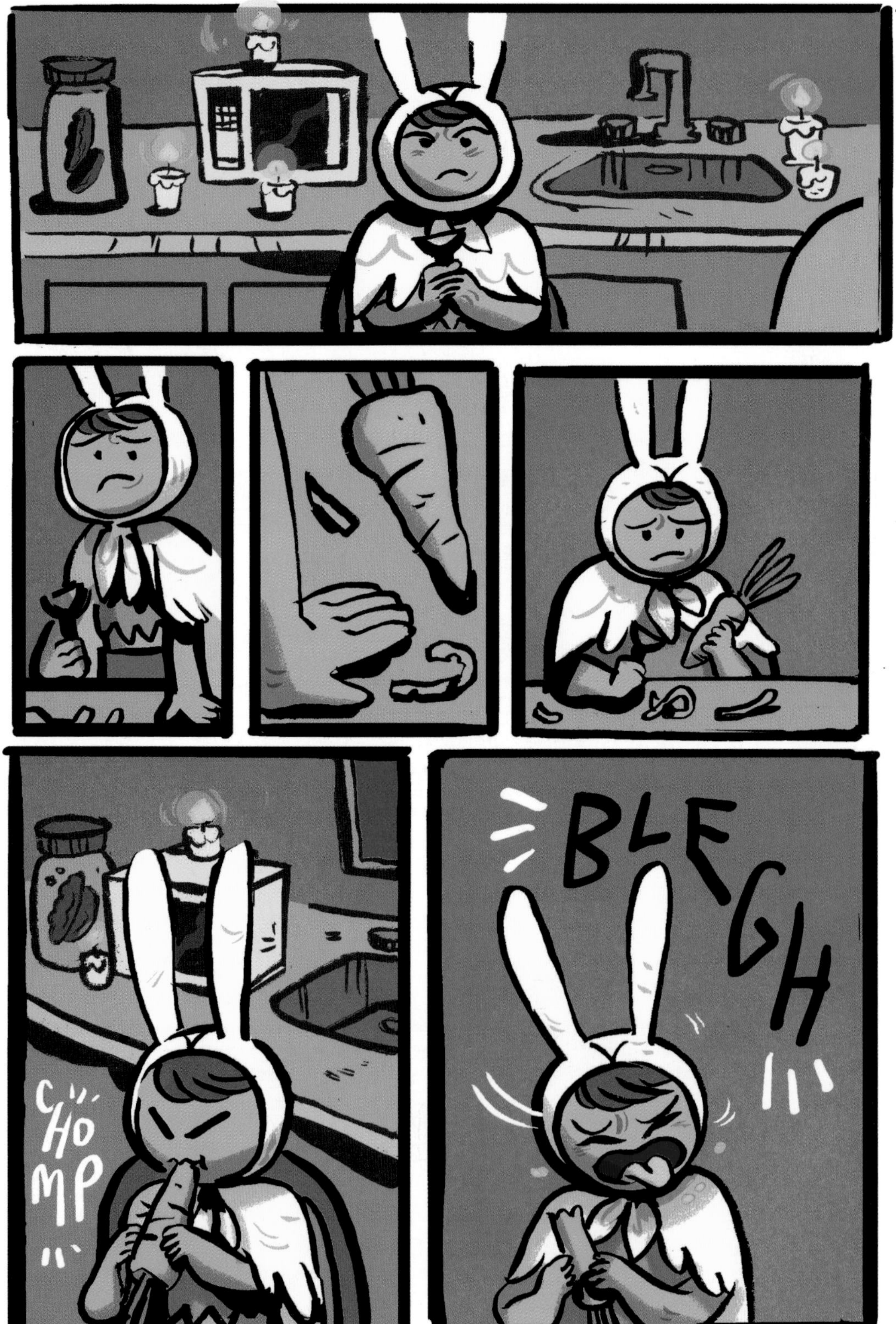
CHOMP
BLEGH

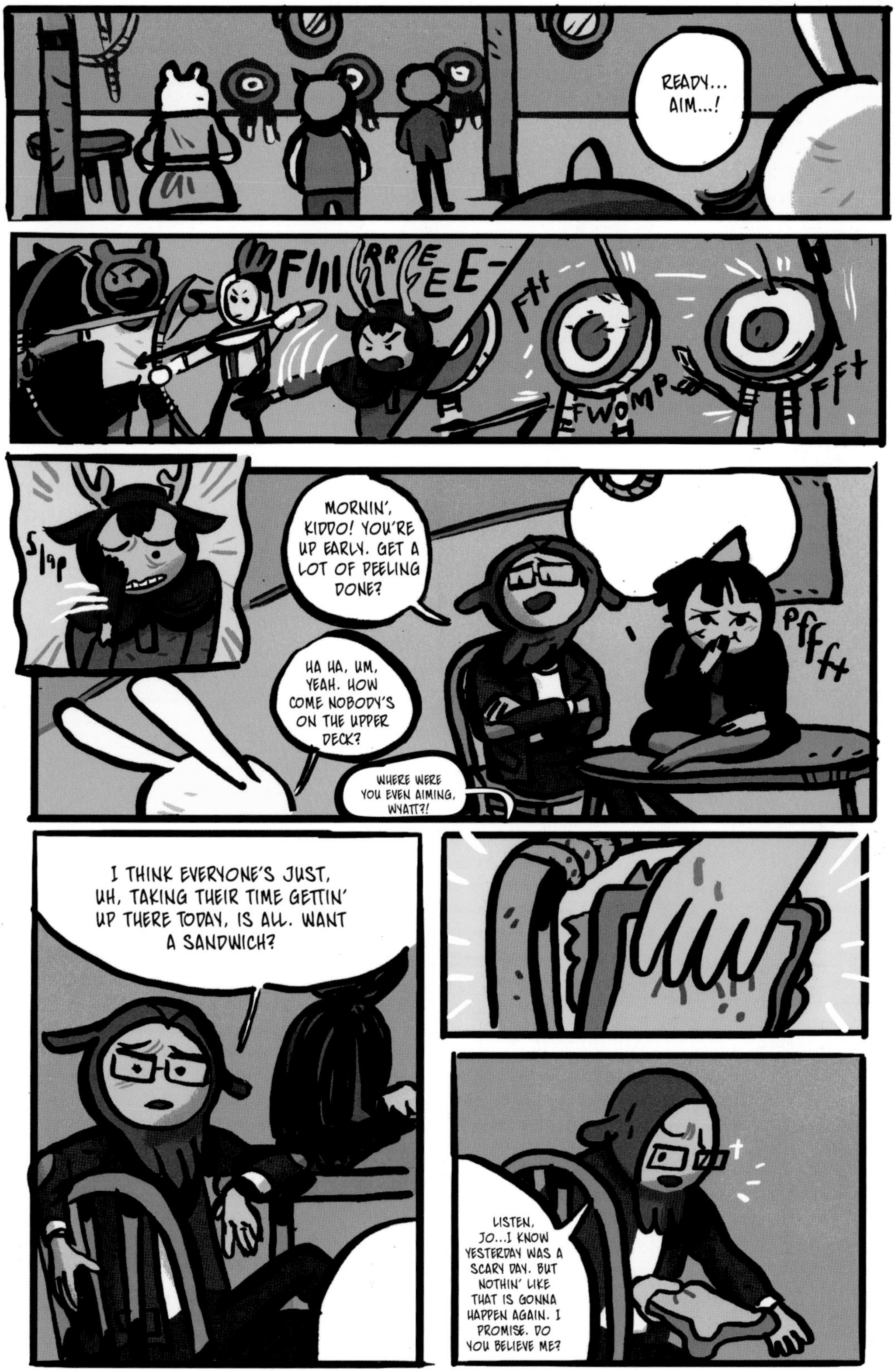
READY... AIM...!
FIIIRRREEE-
FT
FWOMP
FFT
SLAP
MORNIN', KIDDO! YOU'RE UP EARLY. GET A LOT OF PEELING DONE?
PFFFT
HA HA, UM, YEAH. HOW COME NOBODY'S ON THE UPPER DECK?
WHERE WERE YOU EVEN AIMING, WYATT?!
I THINK EVERYONE'S JUST, UH, TAKING THEIR TIME GETTIN' UP THERE TODAY, IS ALL. WANT A SANDWICH?
LISTEN, JO...I KNOW YESTERDAY WAS A SCARY DAY. BUT NOTHIN' LIKE THAT IS GONNA HAPPEN AGAIN. I PROMISE. DO YOU BELIEVE ME?

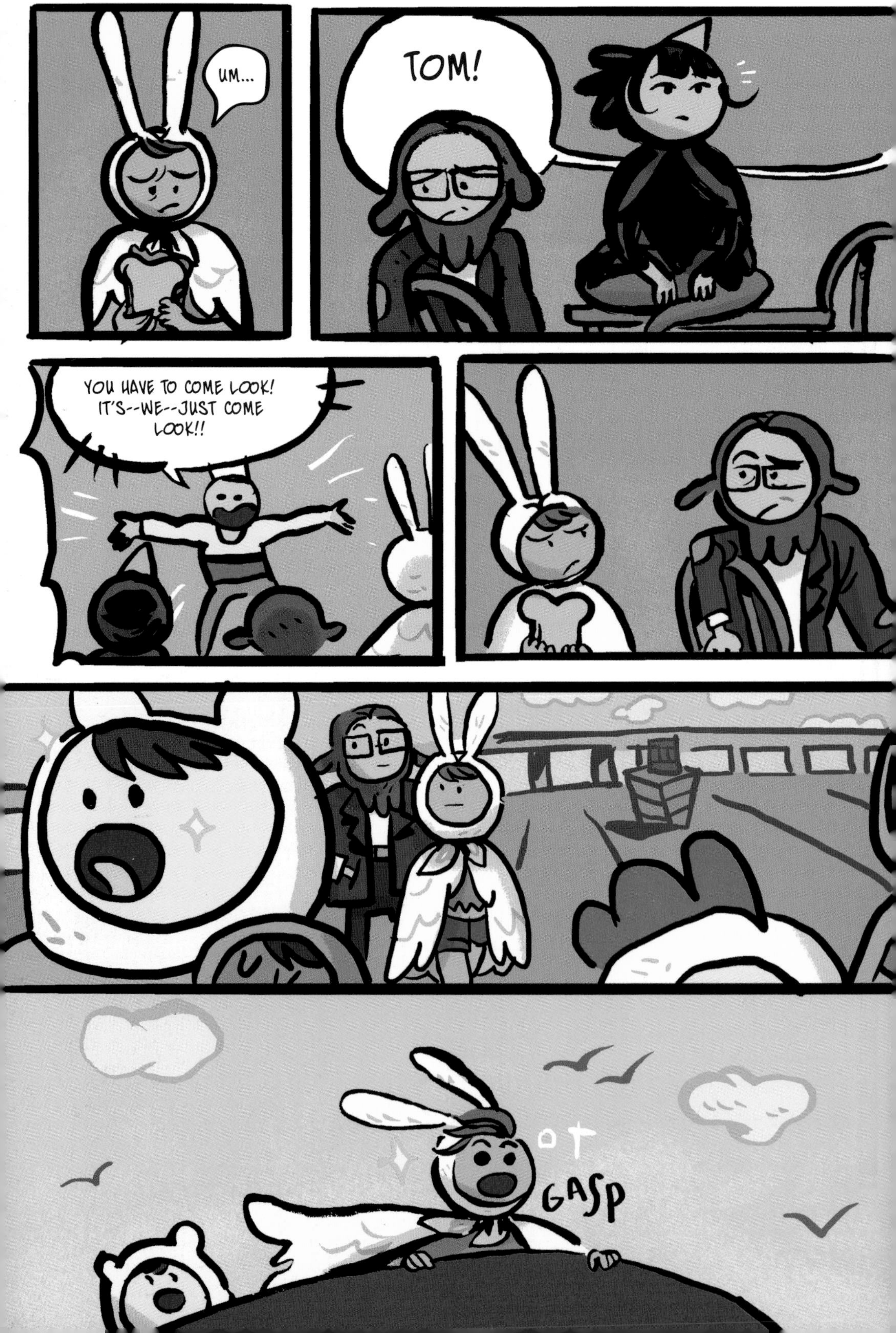
UM...
TOM!
YOU HAVE TO COME LOOK! IT'S--WE--JUST COME LOOK!!
GASP

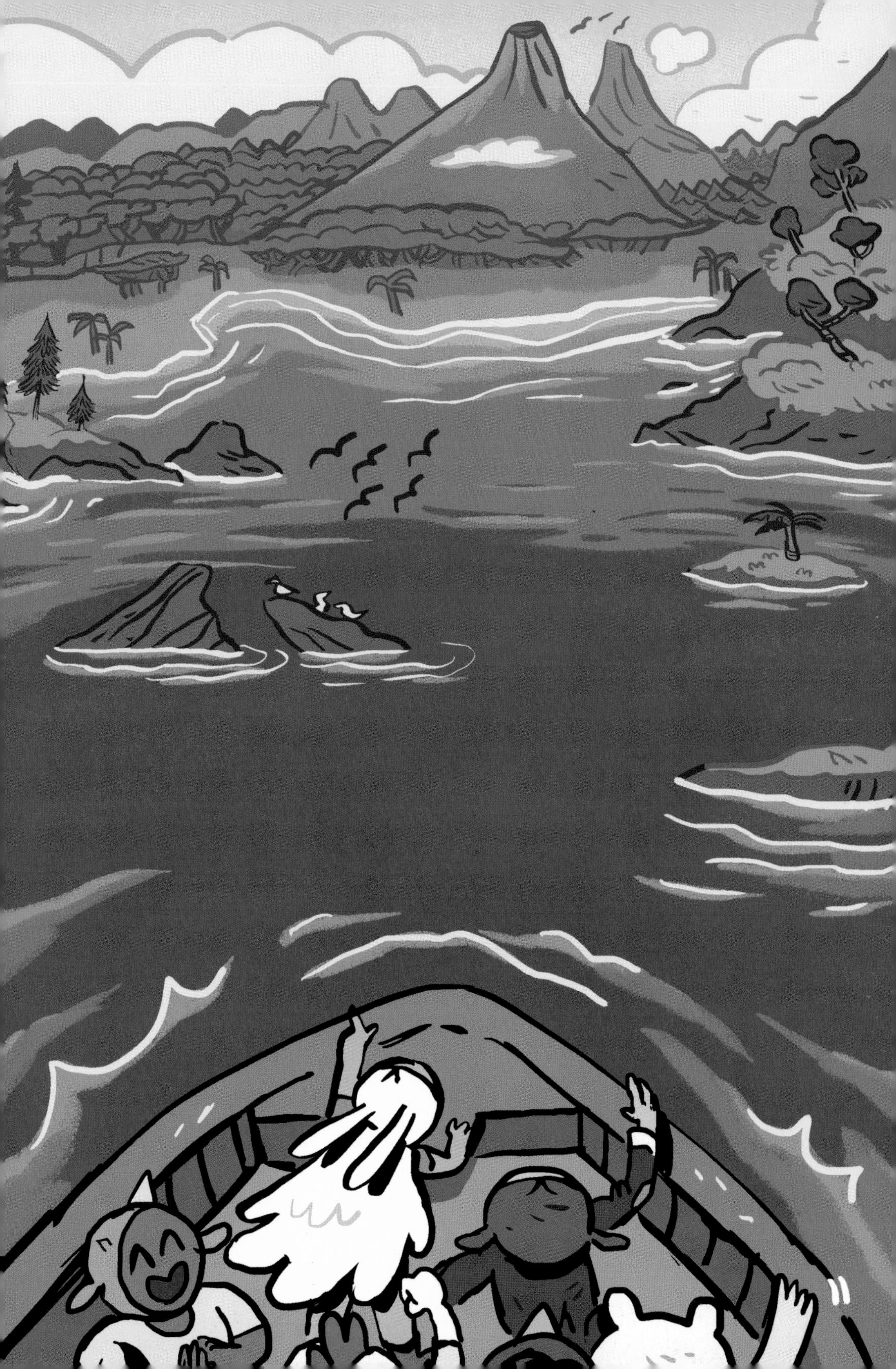

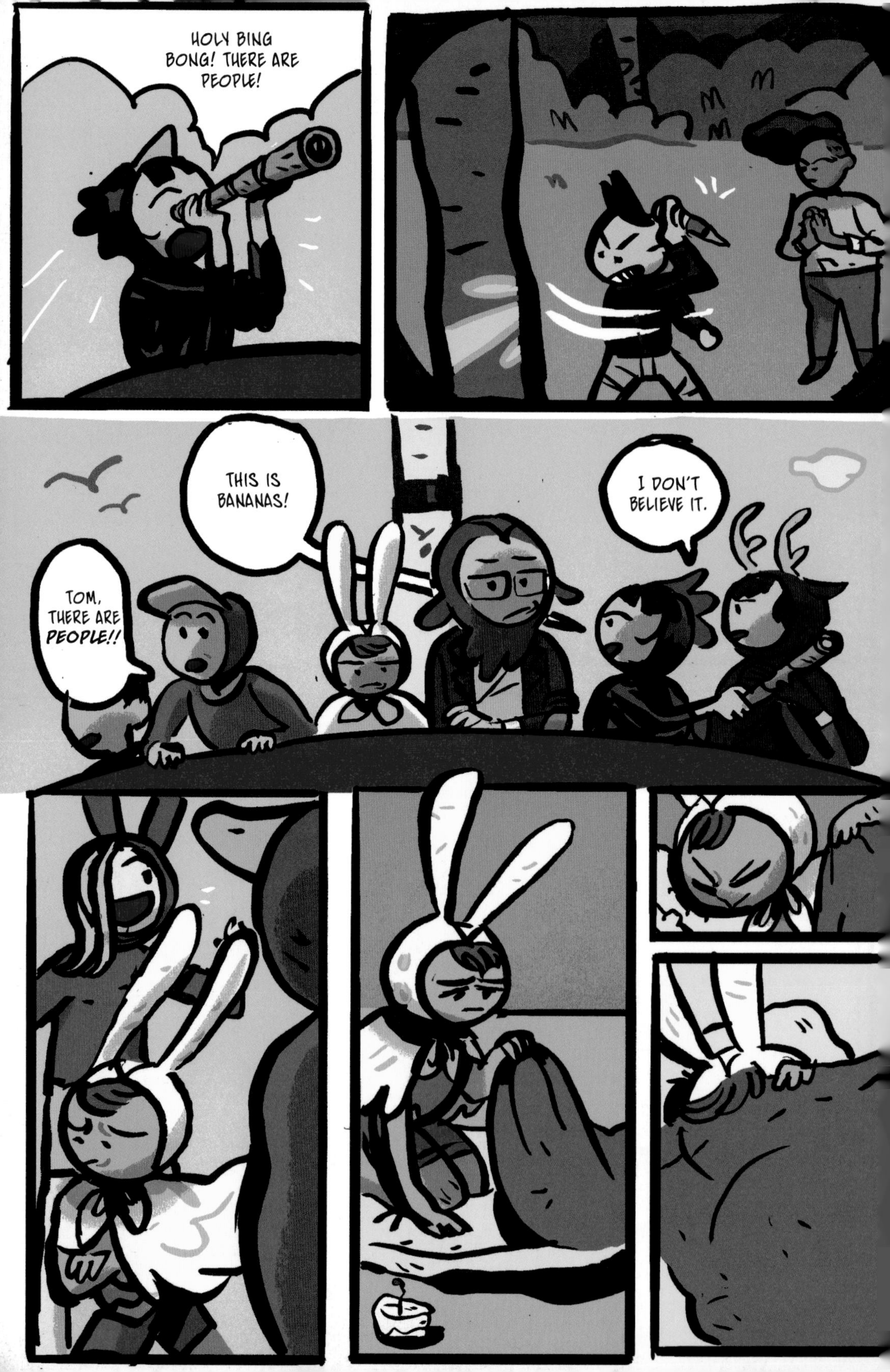
HOLY BING BONG! THERE ARE PEOPLE!
THIS IS BANANAS!
I DON'T BELIEVE IT.
TOM, THERE ARE PEOPLE!!

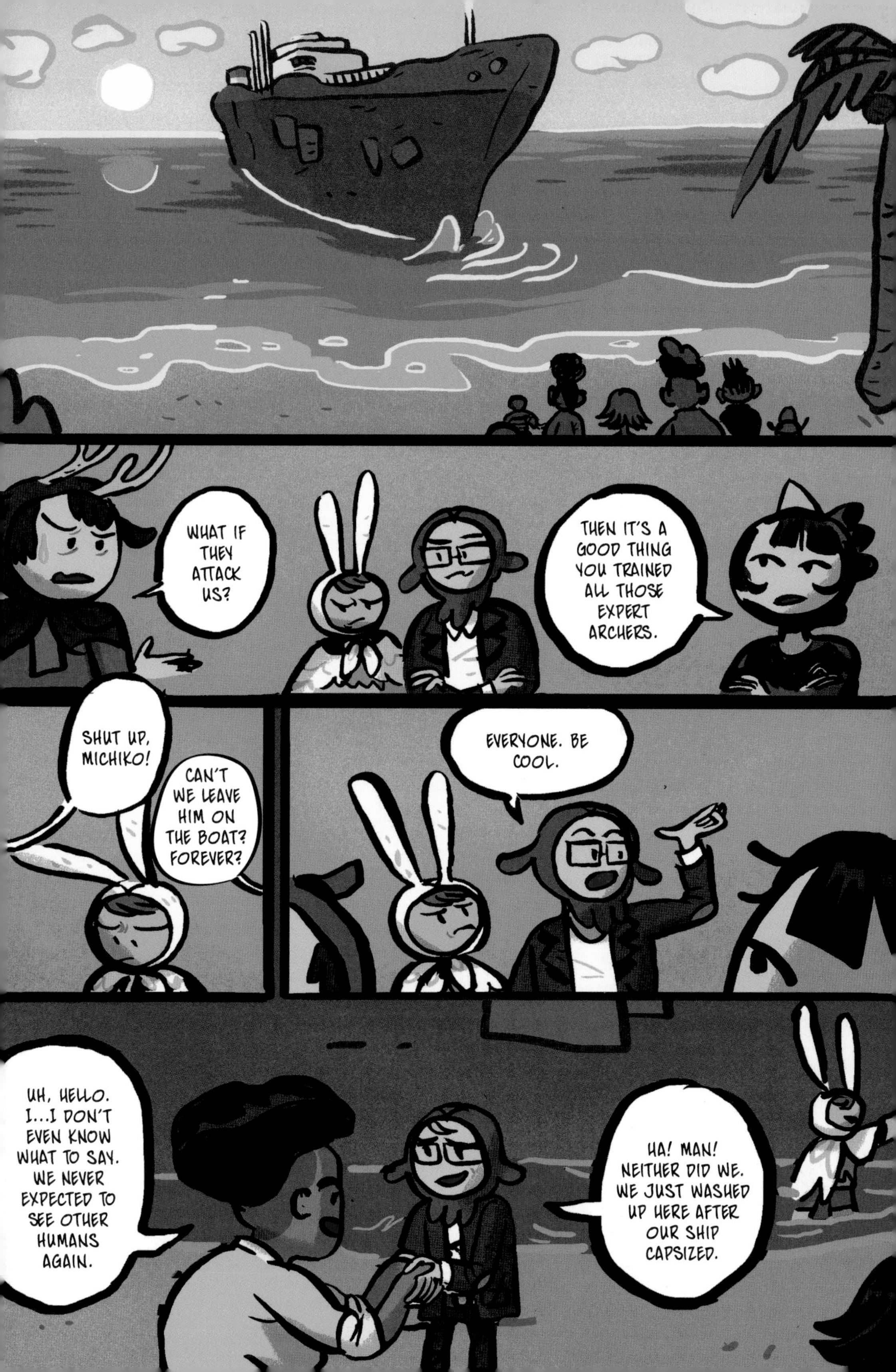
WHAT IF THEY ATTACK US?
THEN IT'S A GOOD THING YOU TRAINED ALL THOSE EXPERT ARCHERS.
SHUT UP, MICHIKO!
CAN'T WE LEAVE HIM ON THE BOAT? FOREVER?
EVERYONE. BE COOL.
UH, HELLO. I...I DON'T EVEN KNOW WHAT TO SAY. WE NEVER EXPECTED TO SEE OTHER HUMANS AGAIN.
HA! MAN! NEITHER DID WE. WE JUST WASHED UP HERE AFTER OUR SHIP CAPSIZED.

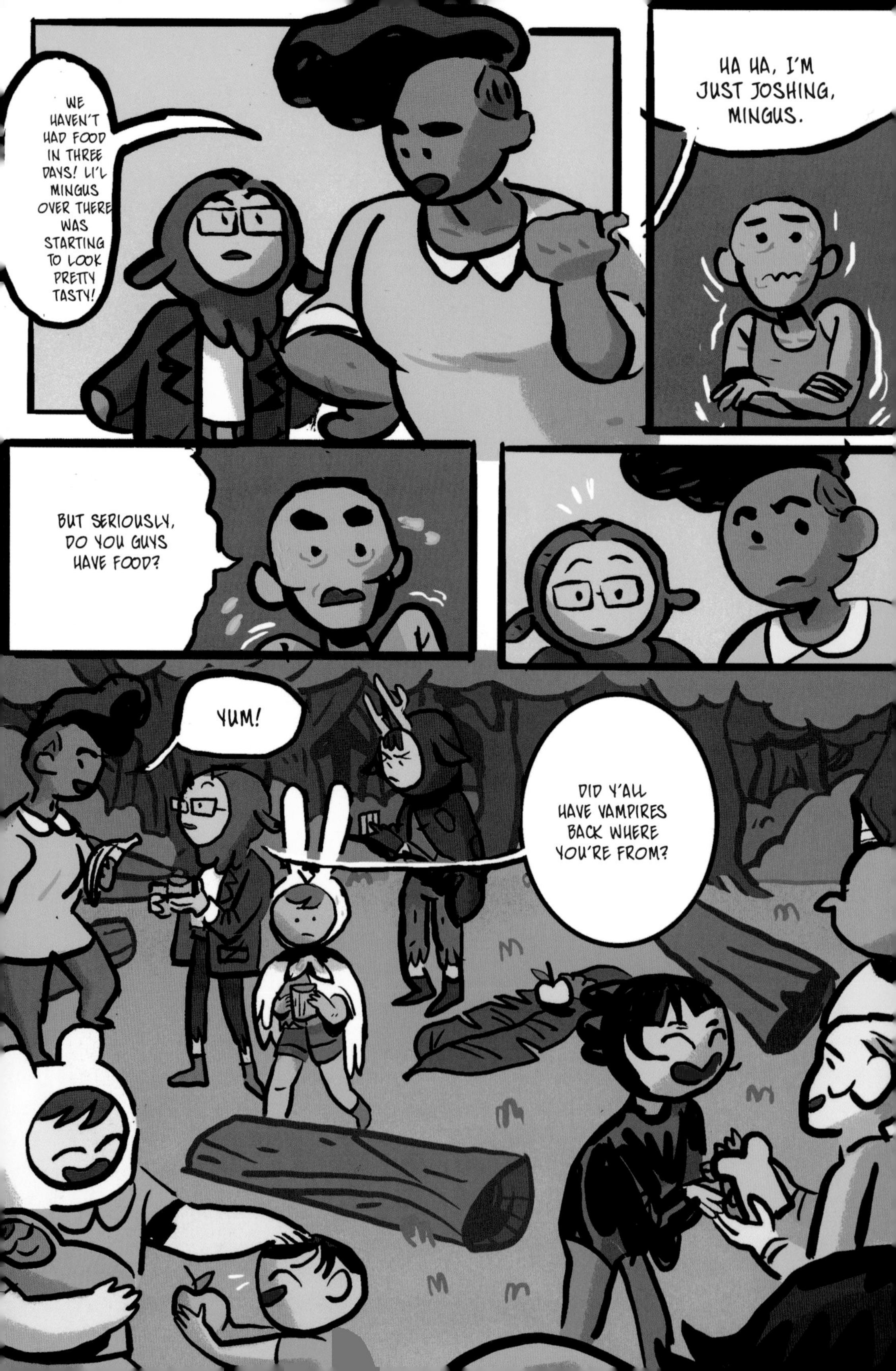
WE HAVEN'T HAD FOOD IN THREE DAYS! LI'L MINGUS OVER THERE WAS STARTING TO LOOK PRETTY TASTY!
HA HA, I'M JUST JOSHING, MINGUS.
BUT SERIOUSLY, DO YOU GUYS HAVE FOOD?
YUM!
DID Y'ALL HAVE VAMPIRES BACK WHERE YOU'RE FROM?

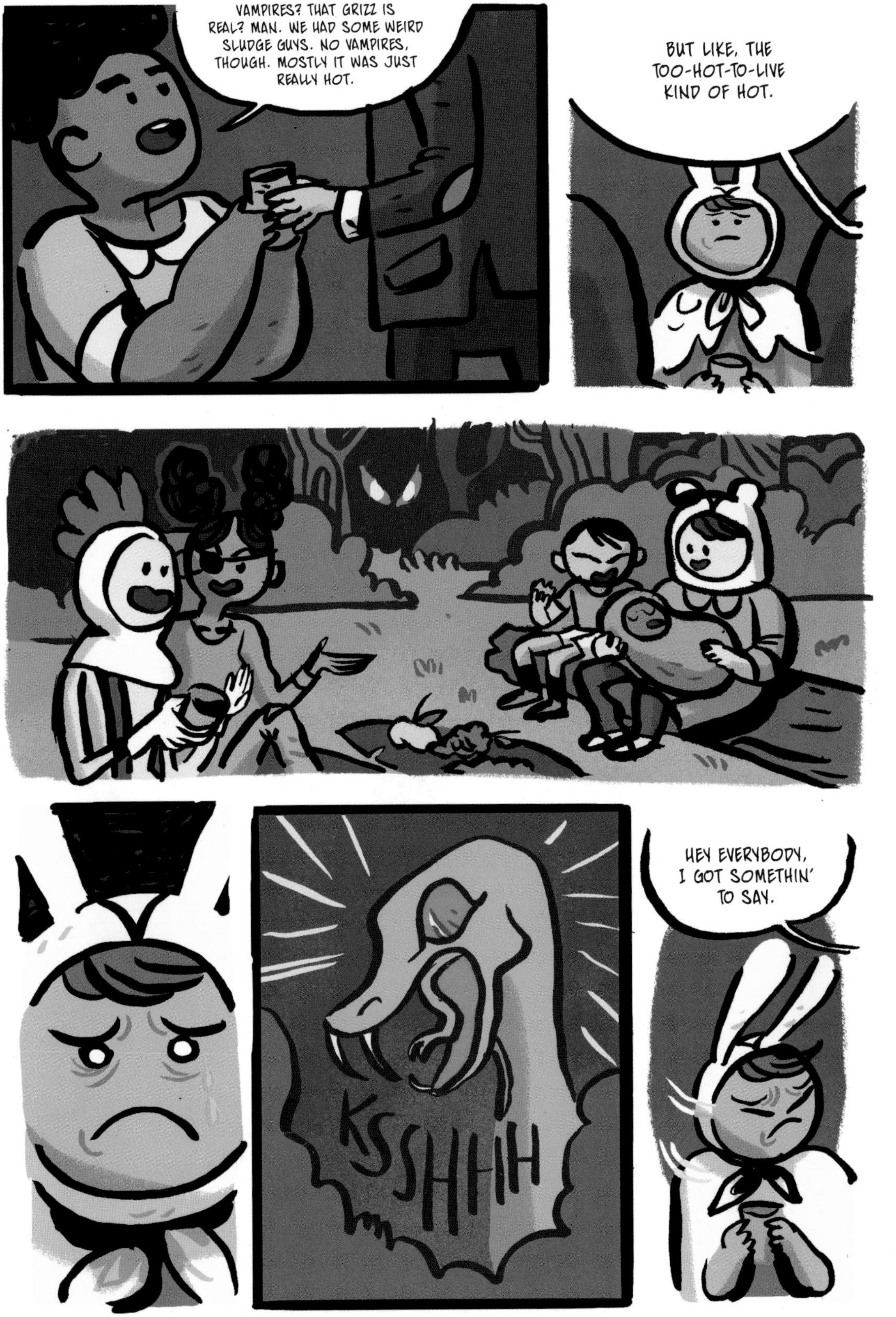
VAMPIRES? THAT GRIZZ IS REAL? MAN. WE HAD SOME WEIRD SLUDGE GUYS. NO VAMPIRES, THOUGH. MOSTLY IT WAS JUST REALLY HOT.
BUT LIKE, THE TOO-HOT-TO-LIVE KIND OF HOT.
KSSHHH
HEY EVERYBODY, I GOT SOMETHIN' TO SAY.

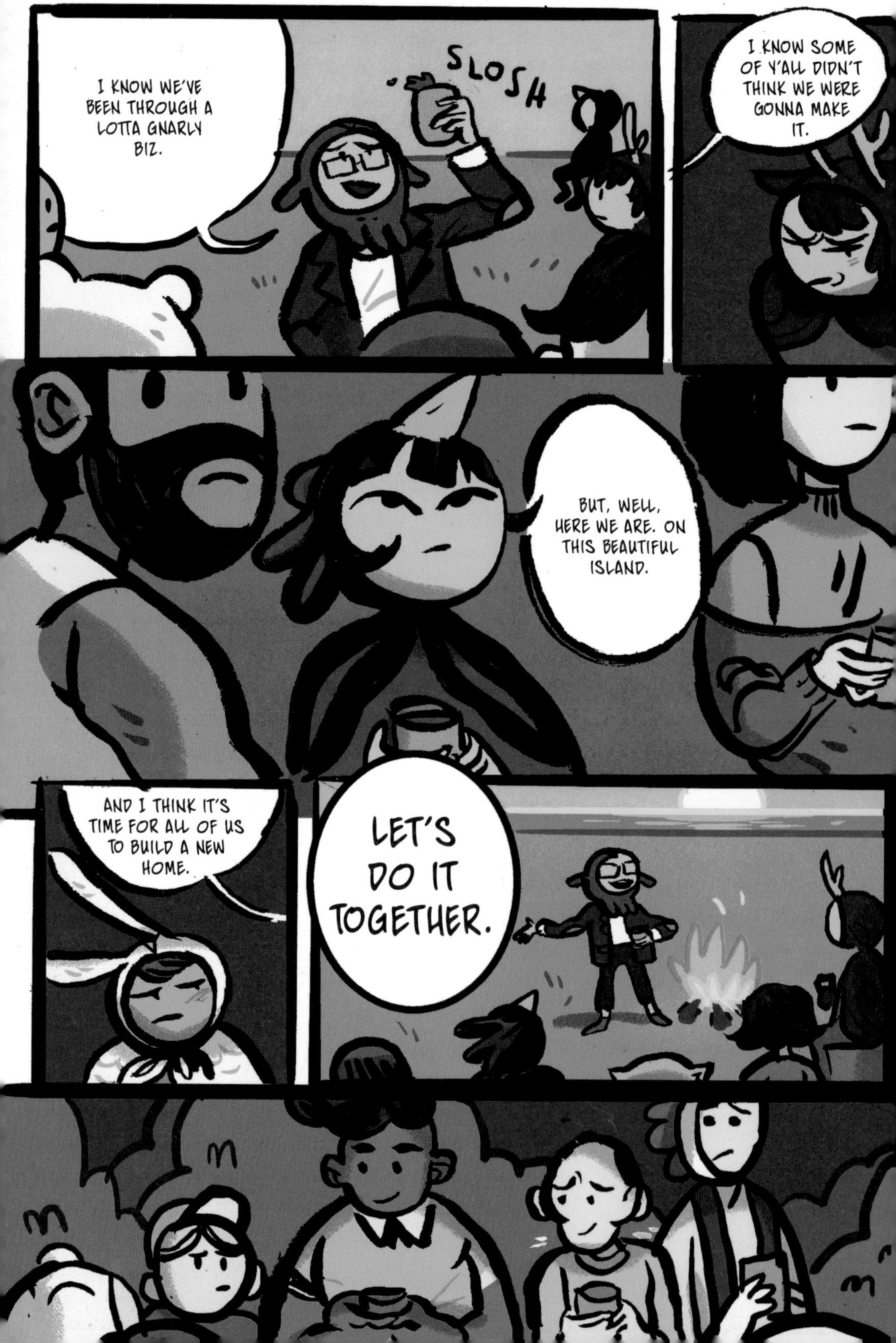
I KNOW WE'VE BEEN THROUGH A LOTTA GNARLY BIZ.
SLOSH
I KNOW SOME OF Y'ALL DIDN'T THINK WE WERE GONNA MAKE IT.
BUT, WELL, HERE WE ARE. ON THIS BEAUTIFUL ISLAND.
AND I THINK IT'S TIME FOR ALL OF US TO BUILD A NEW HOME.
LET'S DO IT TOGETHER.

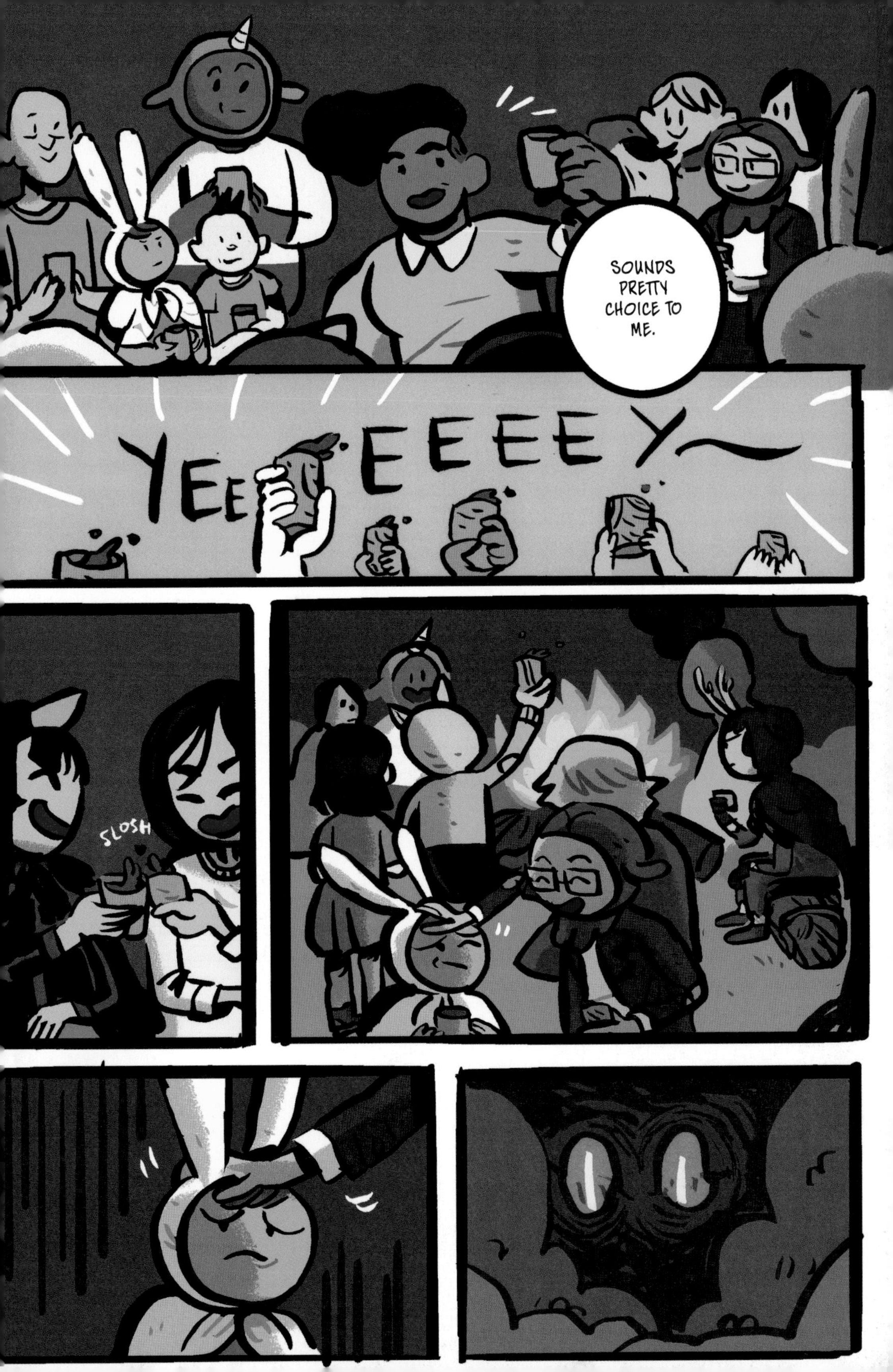
SOUNDS PRETTY CHOICE TO ME.
YEEEEEEY~
SLOSH

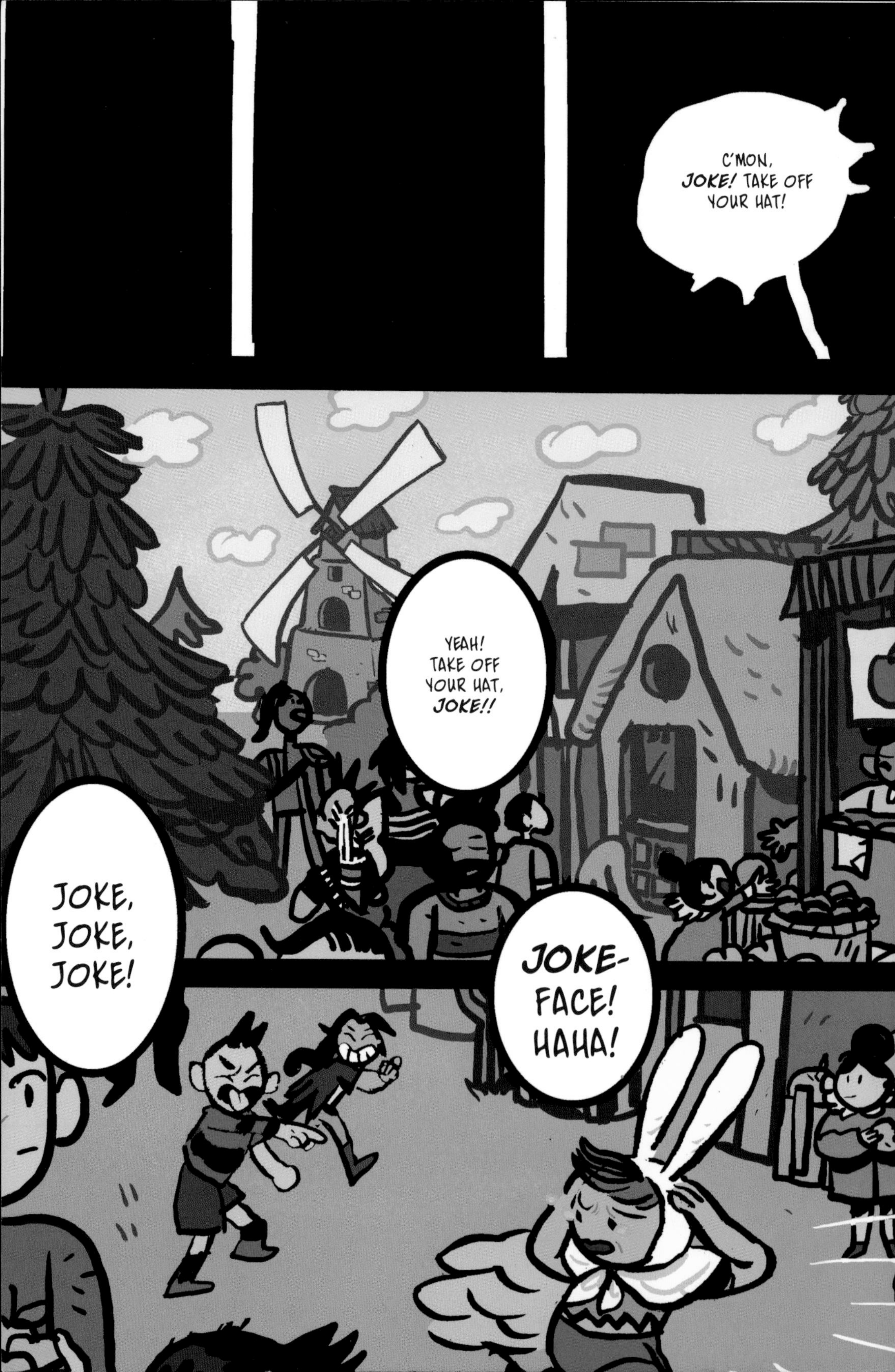
C'MON, JOKE! TAKE OFF YOUR HAT!
YEAH! TAKE OFF YOUR HAT, JOKE!!
JOKE, JOKE, JOKE!
JOKE-FACE! HAHA!

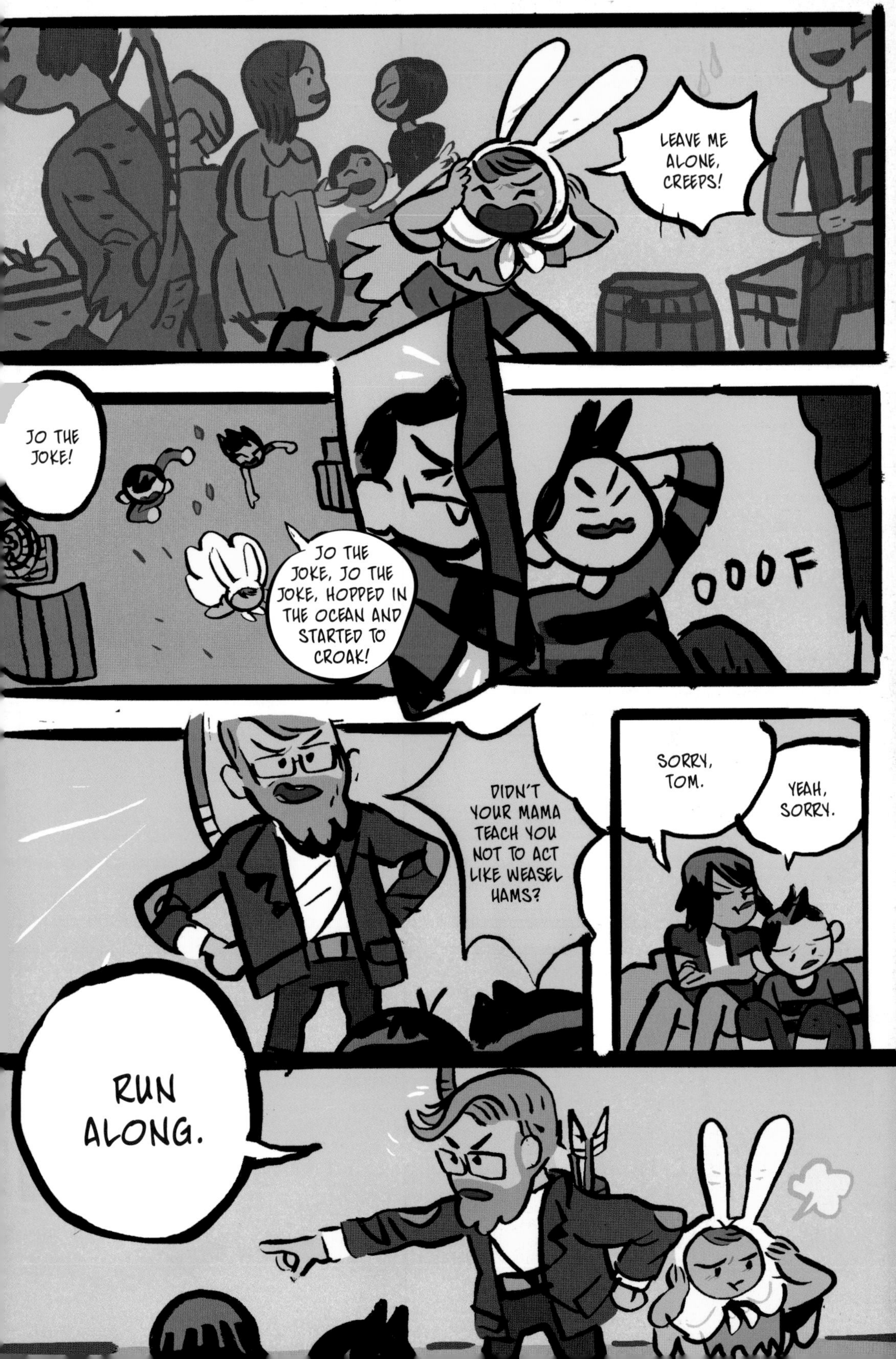
LEAVE ME ALONE, CREEPS!
JO THE JOKE!
JO THE JOKE, JO THE JOKE, HOPPED IN THE OCEAN AND STARTED TO CROAK!
OOOF
DIDN'T YOUR MAMA TEACH YOU NOT TO ACT LIKE WEASEL HAMS?
SORRY, TOM.
YEAH, SORRY.
RUN ALONG.

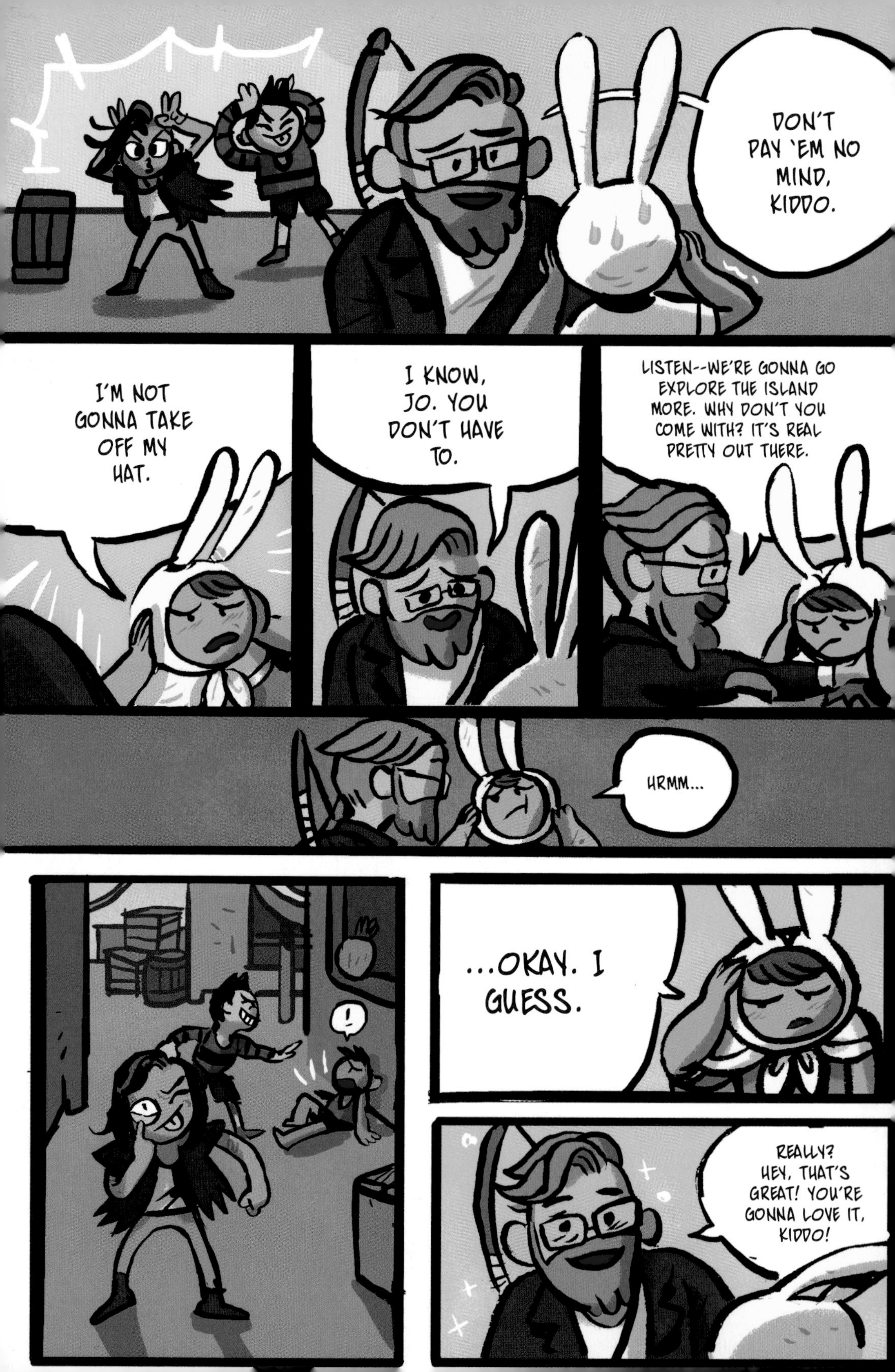
DON'T PAY 'EM NO MIND, KIDDO.
I'M NOT GONNA TAKE OFF MY HAT.
I KNOW, JO. YOU DON'T HAVE TO.
LISTEN--WE'RE GONNA GO EXPLORE THE ISLAND MORE. WHY DON'T YOU COME WITH? IT'S REAL PRETTY OUT THERE.
HRMM...
!
...OKAY. I GUESS.
REALLY? HEY, THAT'S GREAT! YOU'RE GONNA LOVE IT, KIDDO!

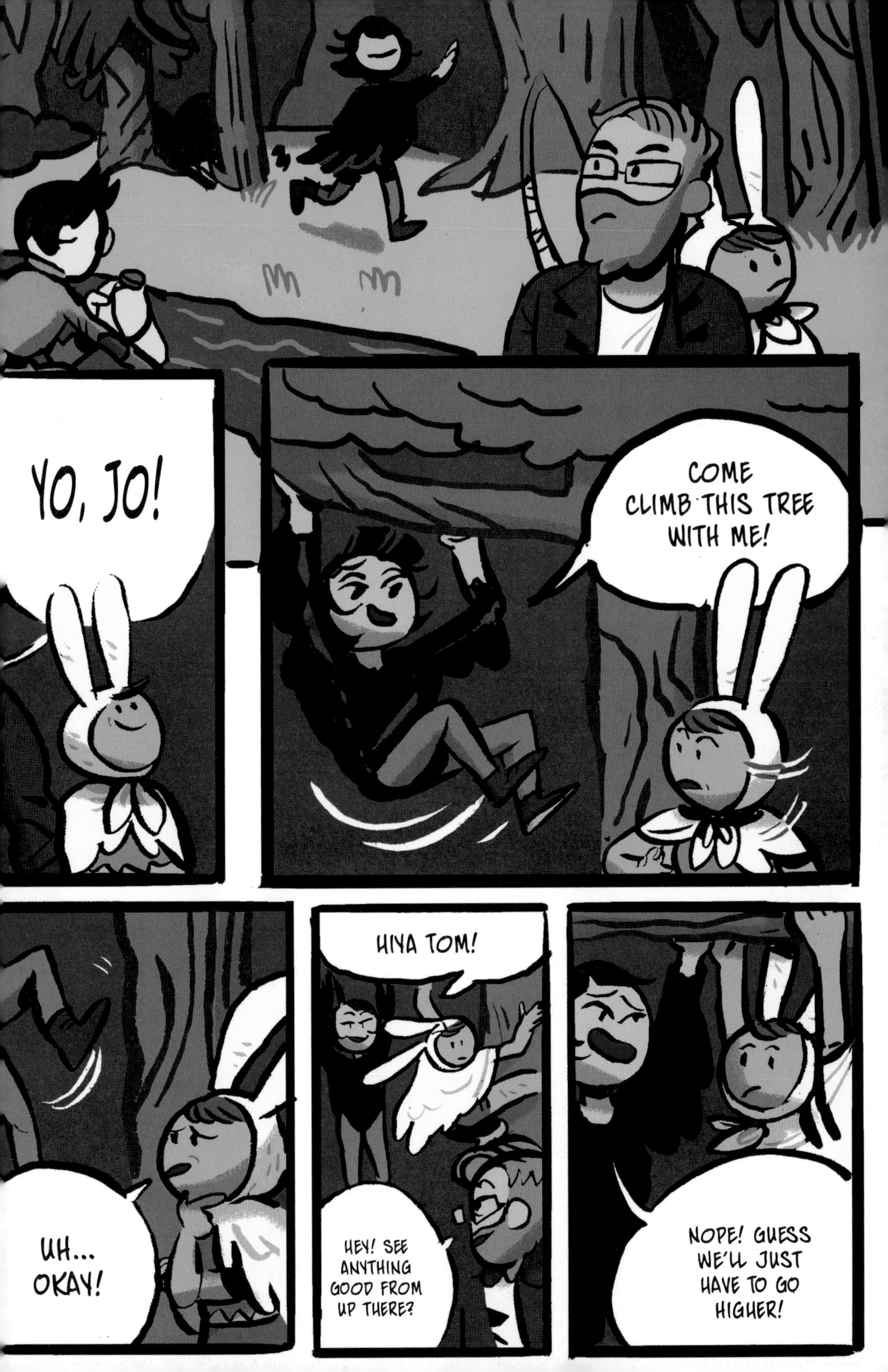
YO, JO!
COME CLIMB THIS TREE WITH ME!
UH... OKAY!
HIYA TOM!
HEY! SEE ANYTHING GOOD FROM UP THERE?
NOPE! GUESS WE'LL JUST HAVE TO GO HIGHER!

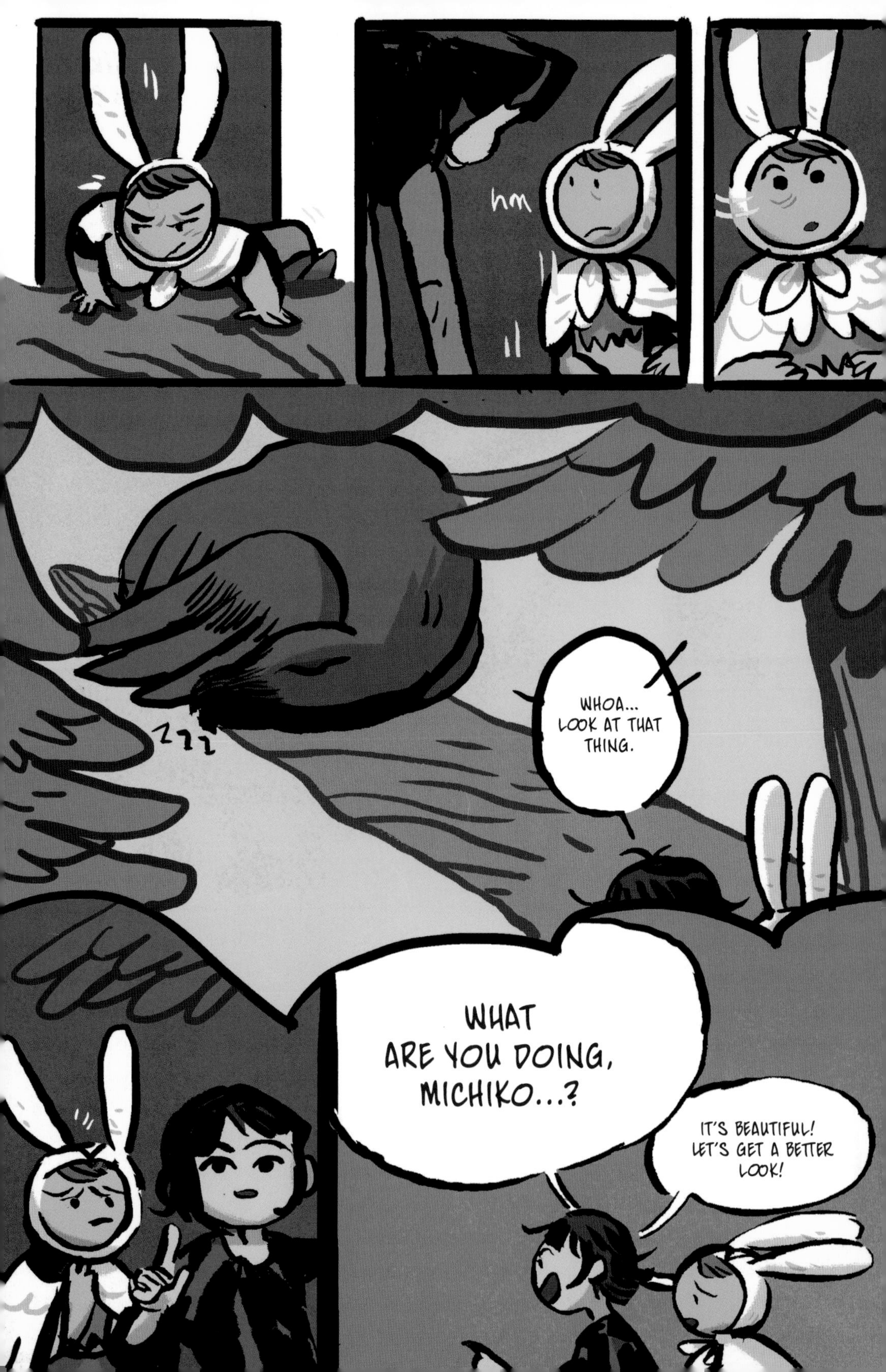
hm
WHOA... LOOK AT THAT THING.
ZZZ
WHAT ARE YOU DOING, MICHIKO...?
IT'S BEAUTIFUL! LET'S GET A BETTER LOOK!

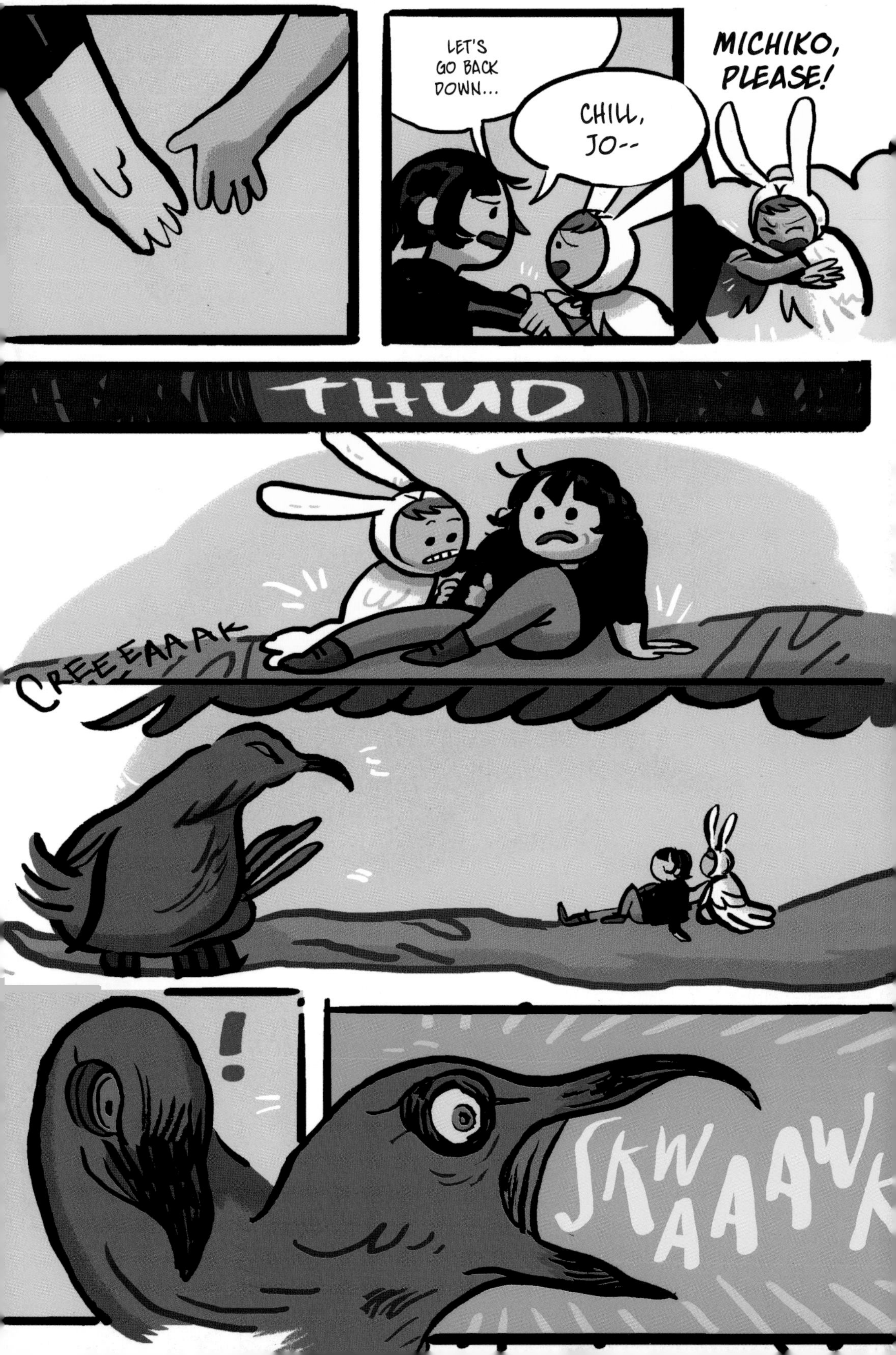
LET'S GO BACK DOWN...
CHILL, JO--
MICHIKO, PLEASE!
THUD
CREEEAAAK
!
SKWAAAAWK

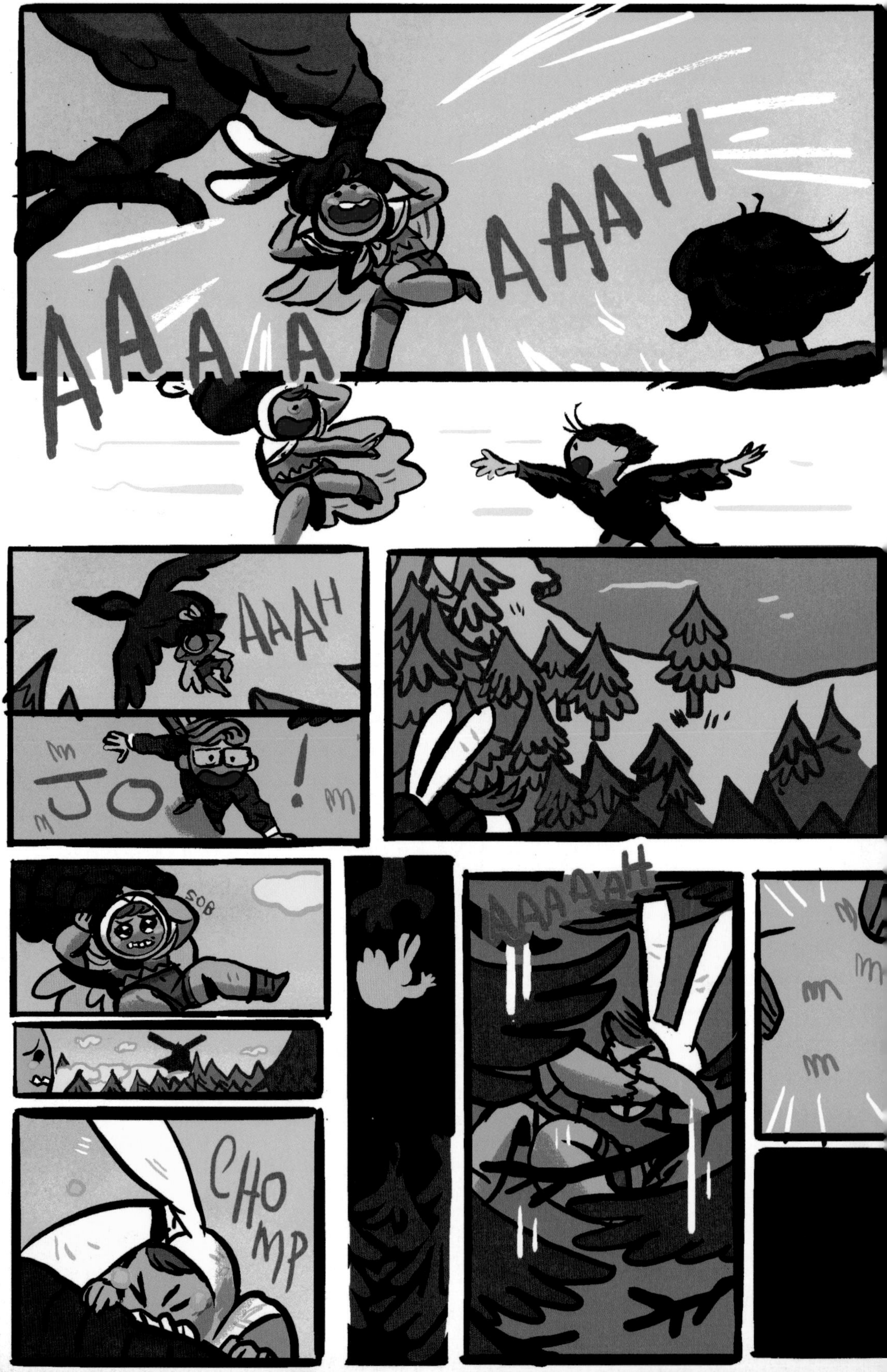

AAAAAAAAH
AAAH
JO!
SOB
AAAAAH
CHOMP

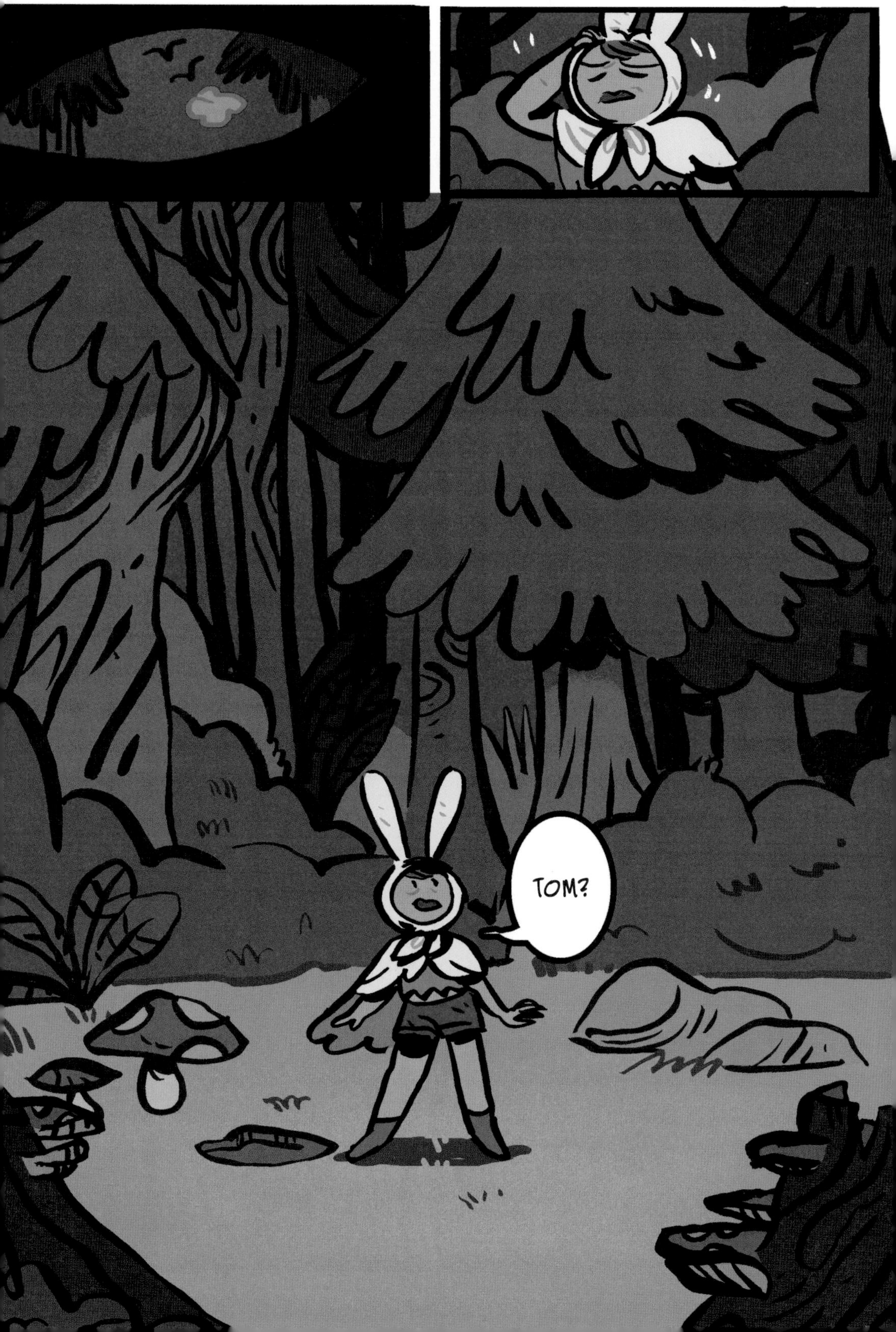
TOM?

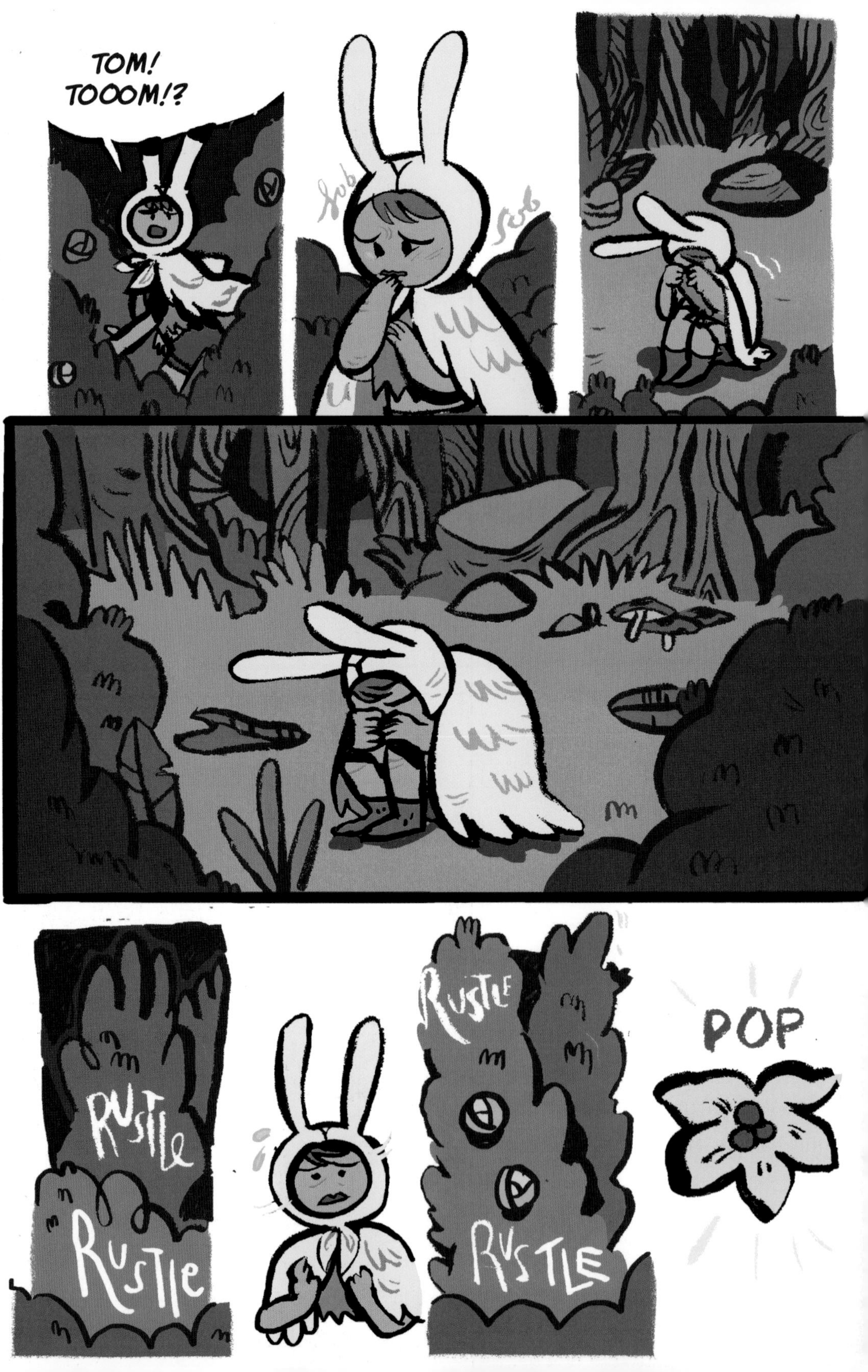
TOM!
TOOOM!?
Sob
Sob
RUSTLE
RUSTLE
RUSTLE
RUSTLE
POP

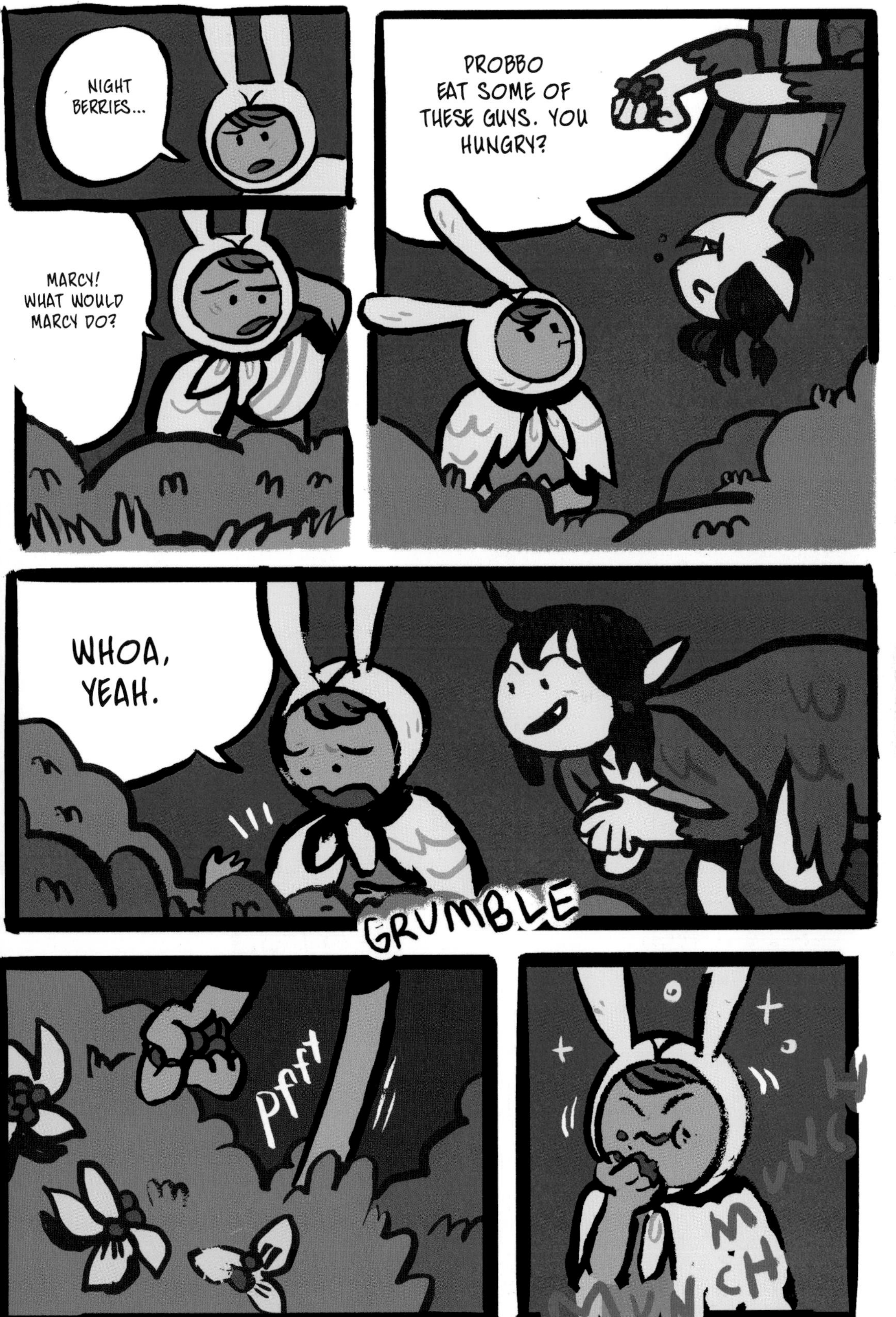

NIGHT BERRIES...
MARCY! WHAT WOULD MARCY DO?
PROBBO EAT SOME OF THESE GUYS. YOU HUNGRY?
WHOA, YEAH.
GRUMBLE
pfft
MUNCH
MUNCH

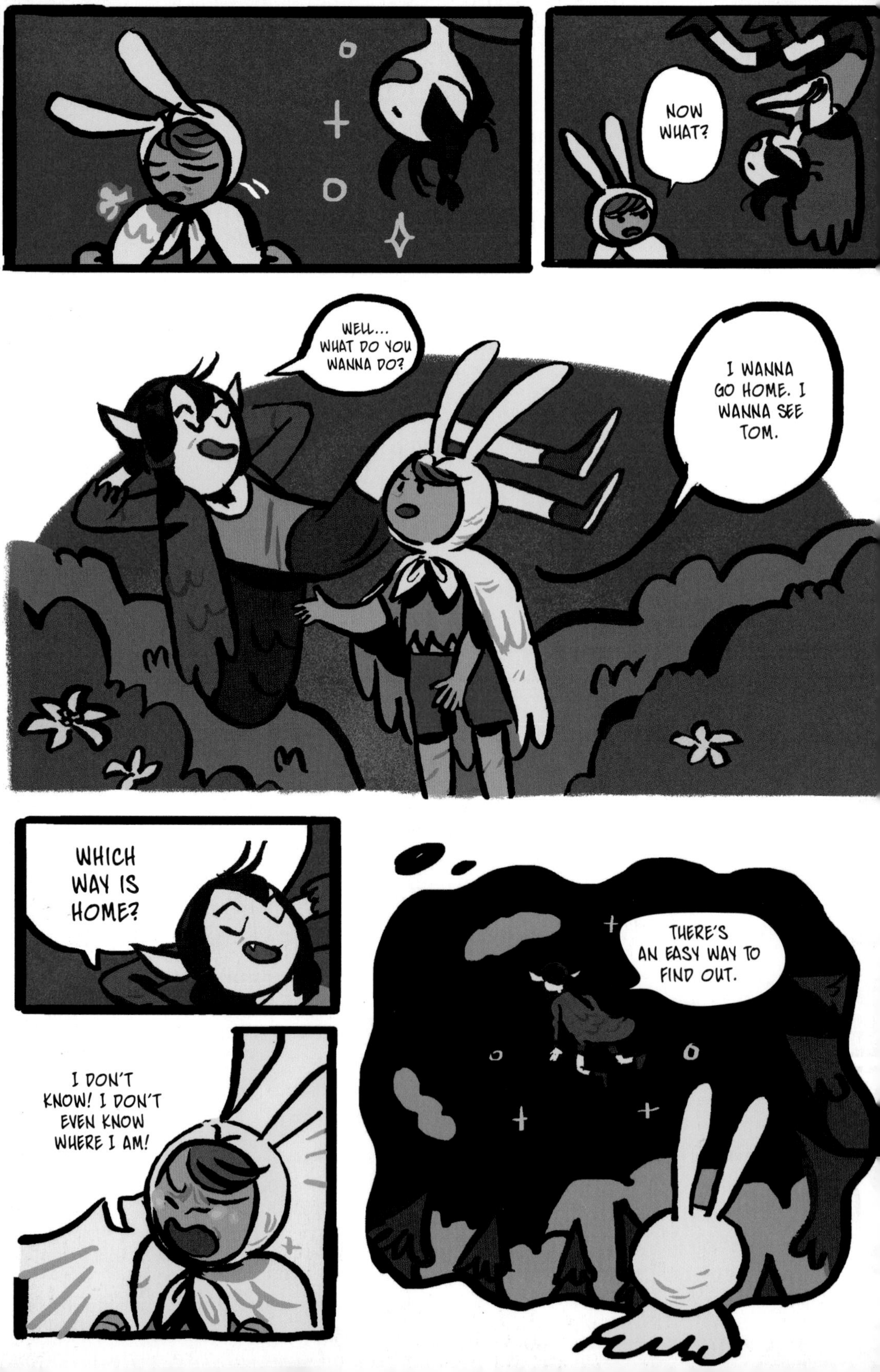
NOW WHAT?
WELL... WHAT DO YOU WANNA DO?
I WANNA GO HOME. I WANNA SEE TOM.
WHICH WAY IS HOME?
I DON'T KNOW! I DON'T EVEN KNOW WHERE I AM!
THERE'S AN EASY WAY TO FIND OUT.

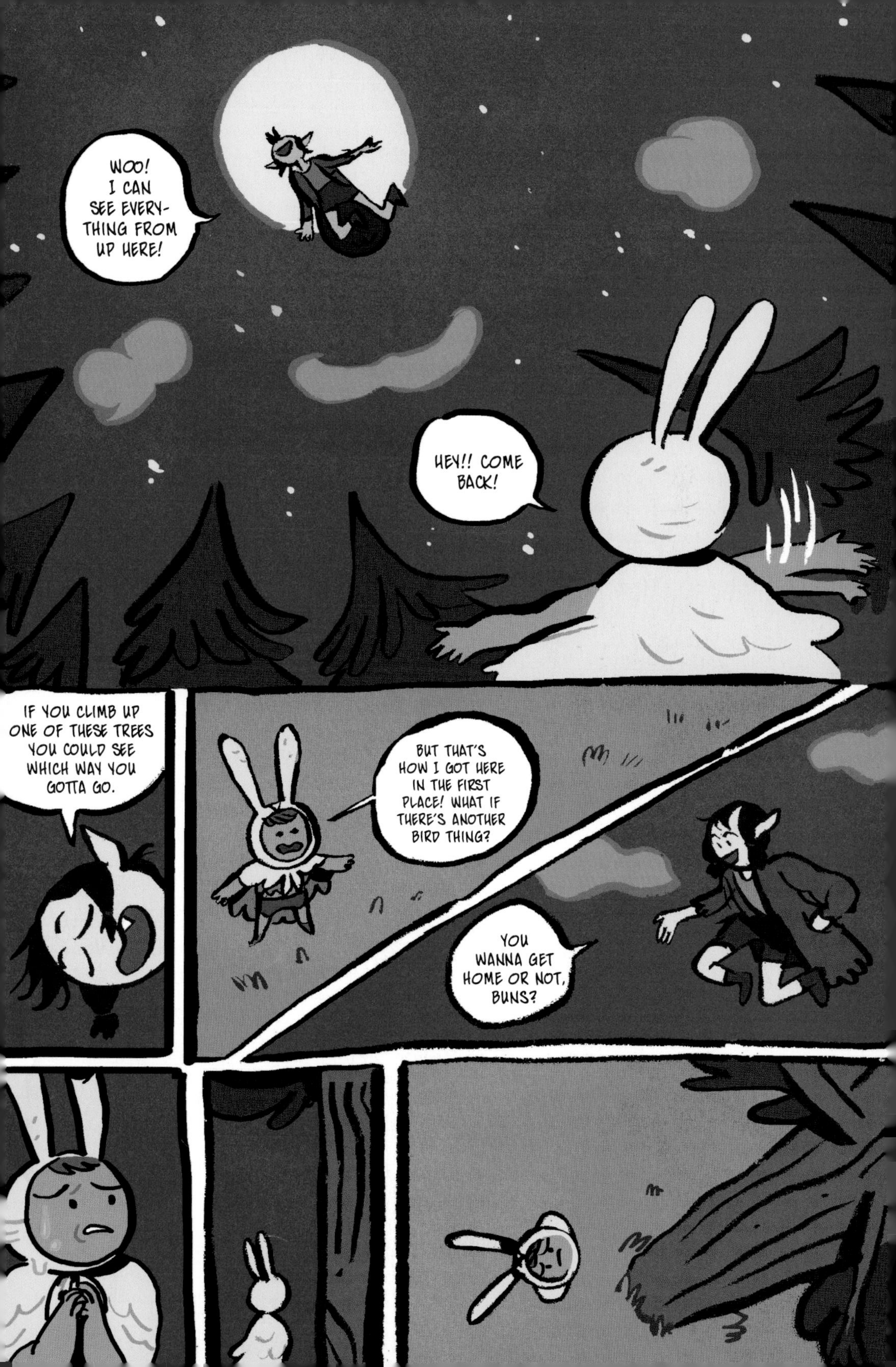
WOO! I CAN SEE EVERY-THING FROM UP HERE!
HEY!! COME BACK!
IF YOU CLIMB UP ONE OF THESE TREES YOU COULD SEE WHICH WAY YOU GOTTA GO.
BUT THAT'S HOW I GOT HERE IN THE FIRST PLACE! WHAT IF THERE'S ANOTHER BIRD THING?
YOU WANNA GET HOME OR NOT, BUNS?

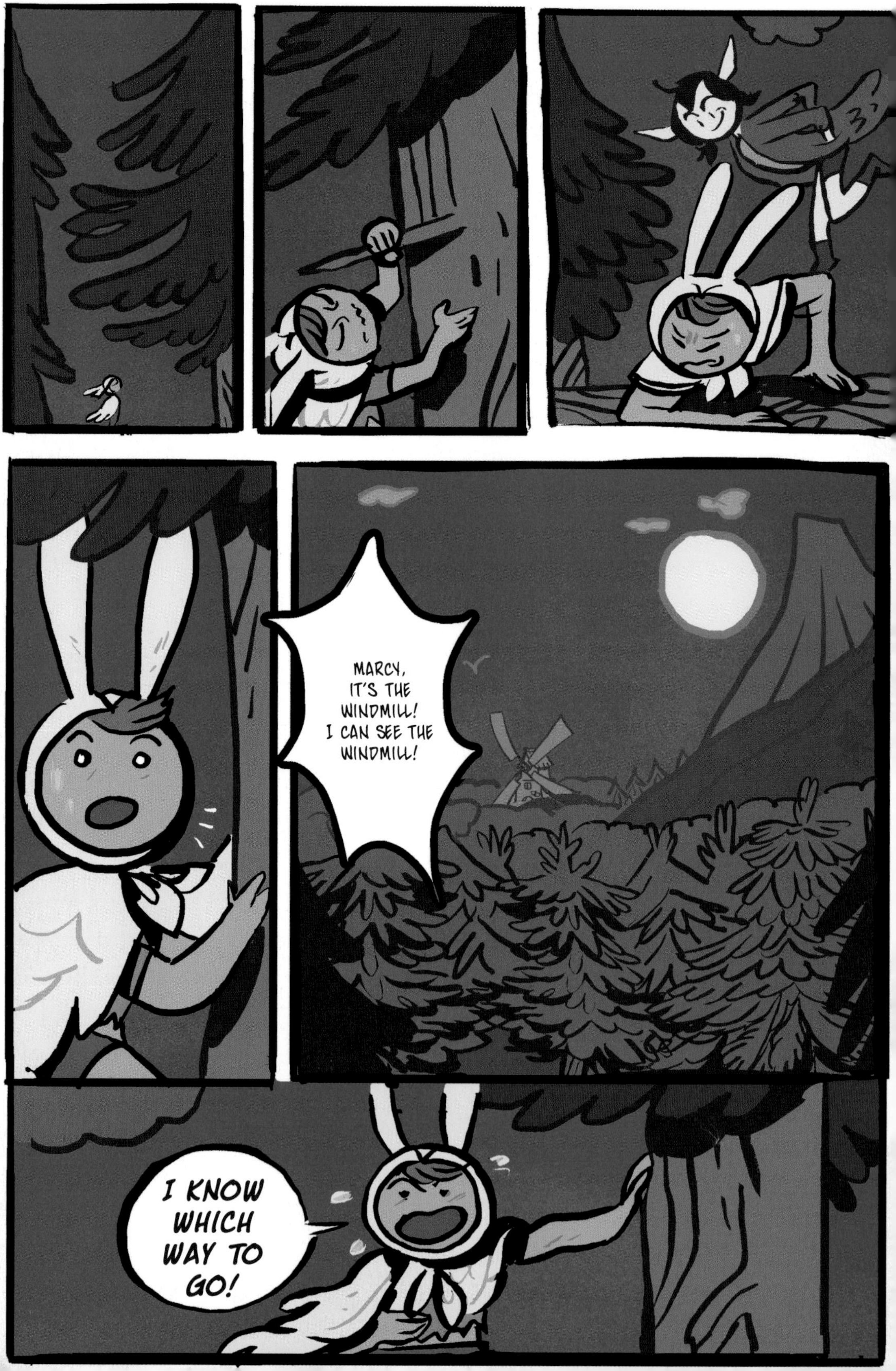
MARCY, IT'S THE WINDMILL! I CAN SEE THE WINDMILL!
I KNOW WHICH WAY TO GO!

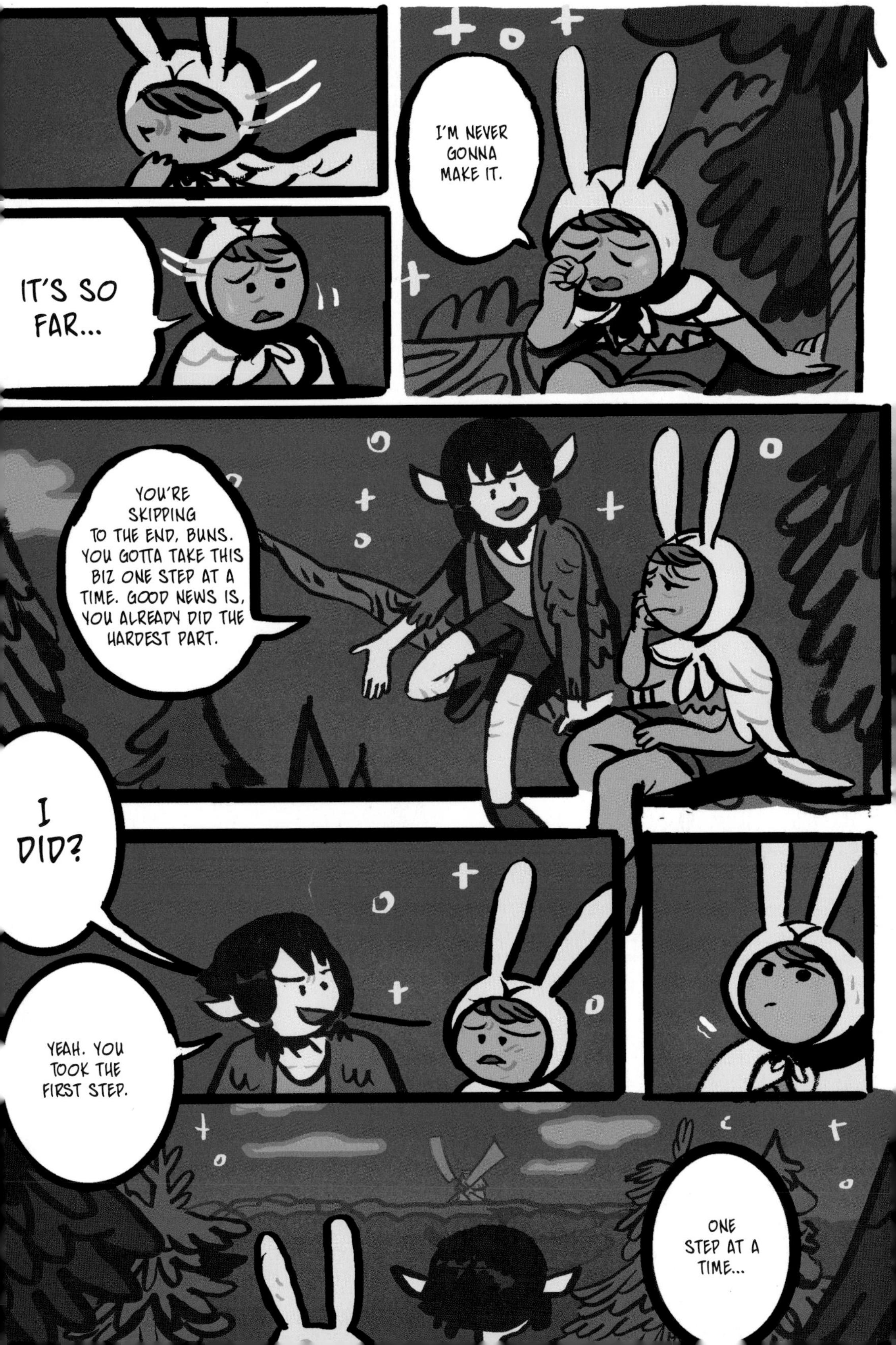
I'M NEVER GONNA MAKE IT.
IT'S SO FAR...
YOU'RE SKIPPING TO THE END, BUNS. YOU GOTTA TAKE THIS BIZ ONE STEP AT A TIME. GOOD NEWS IS, YOU ALREADY DID THE HARDEST PART.
I DID?
YEAH. YOU TOOK THE FIRST STEP.
ONE STEP AT A TIME...

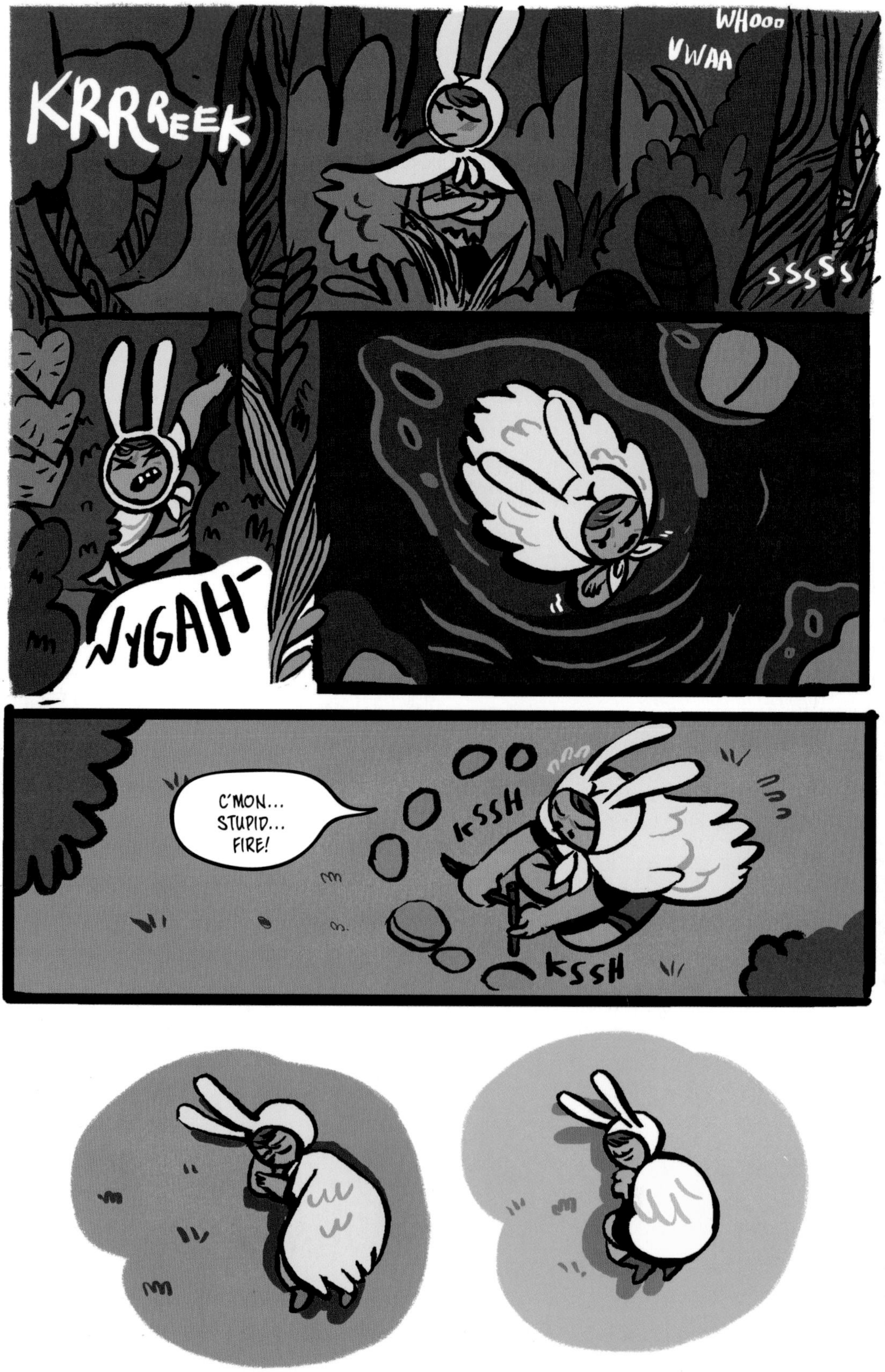
KRRREEK
WHOooo
VWAA
SSSSS
NYGAH
C'MON... STUPID... FIRE!
KSSH
KSSH

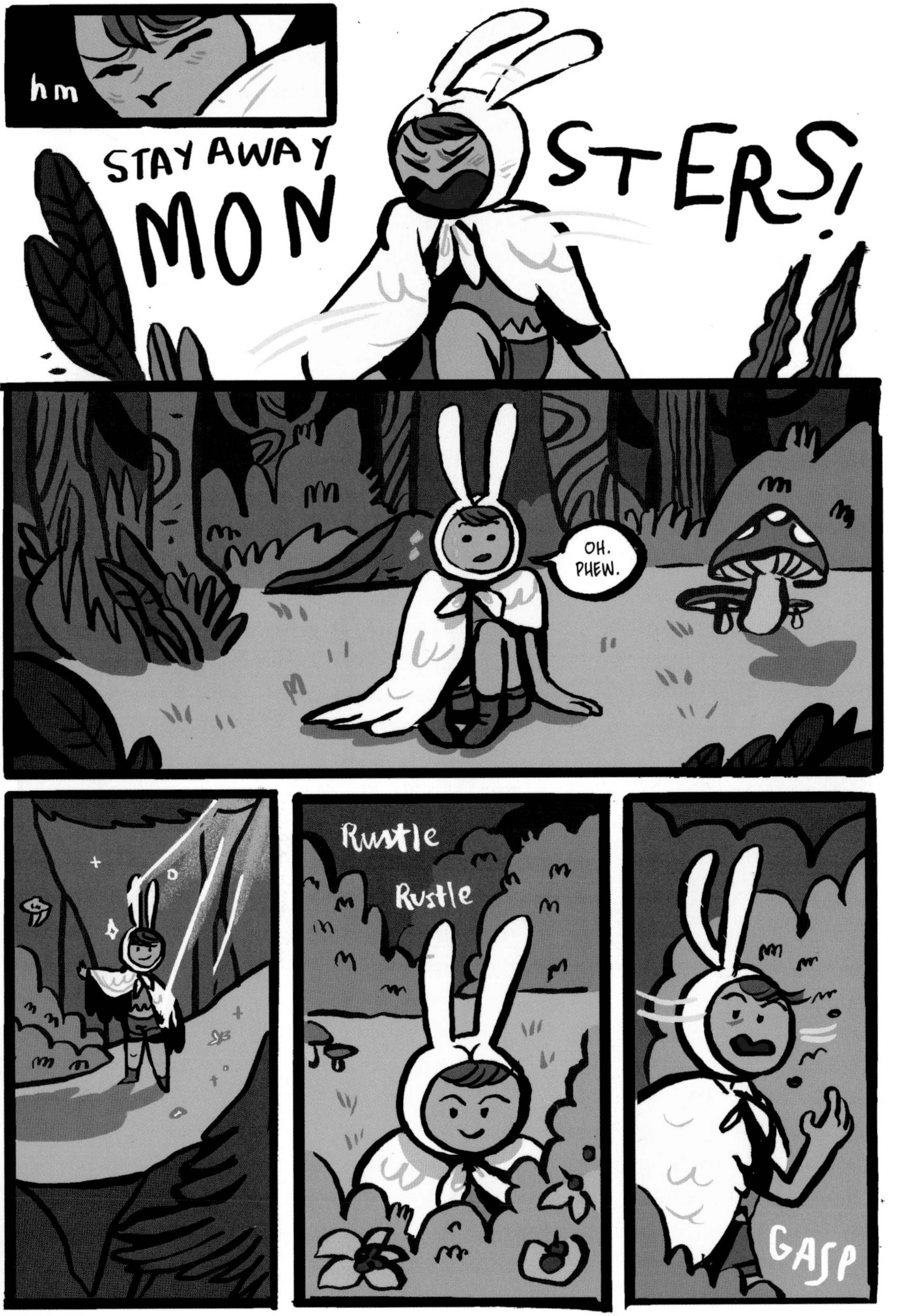
hm
STAY AWAY MONSTERS!
OH. PHEW.
Rustle
Rustle
GASP

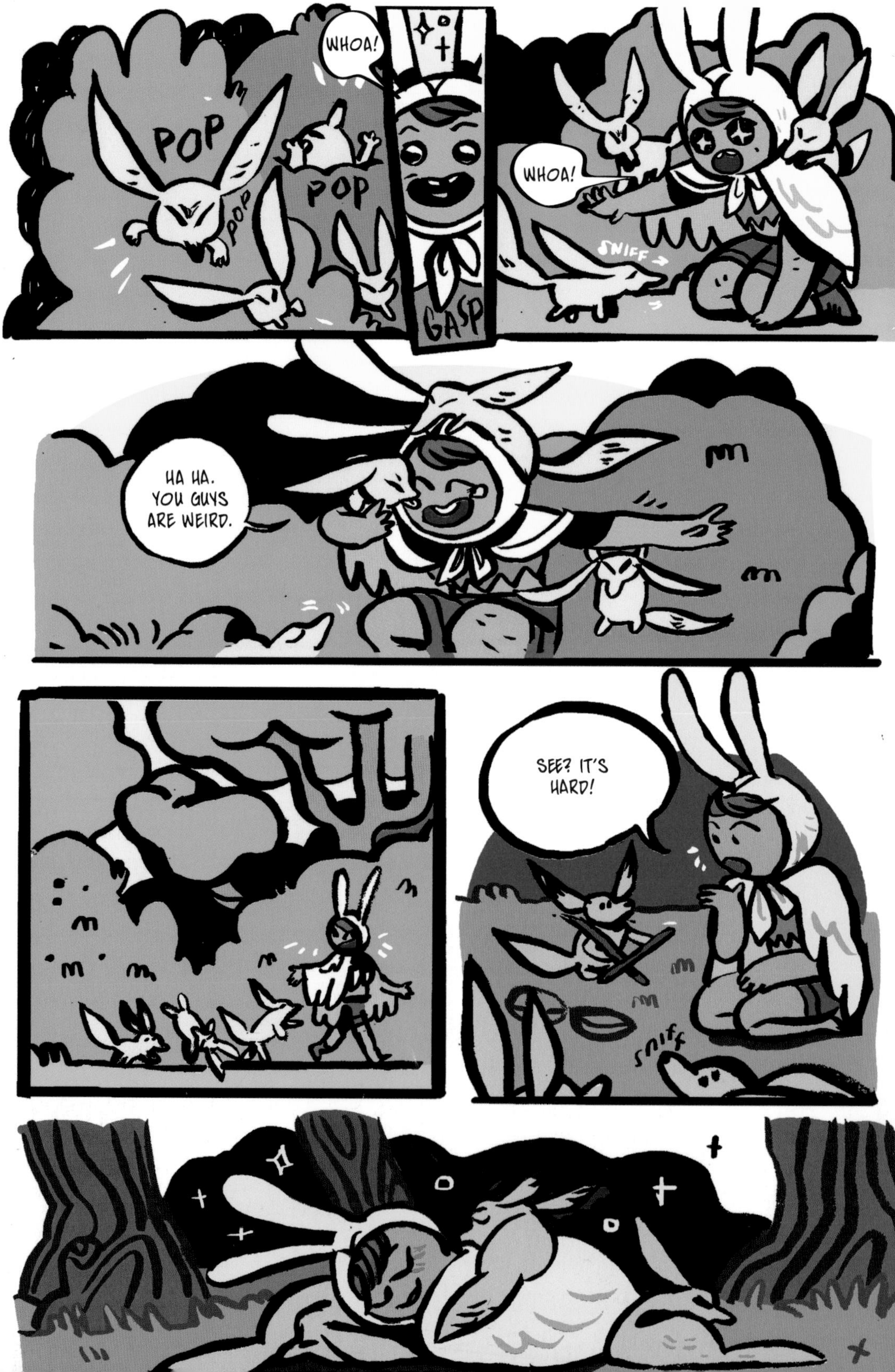
POP
POP
POP
WHOA!
GASP
WHOA!
SNIFF
HA HA. YOU GUYS ARE WEIRD.
SEE? IT'S HARD!
sniff

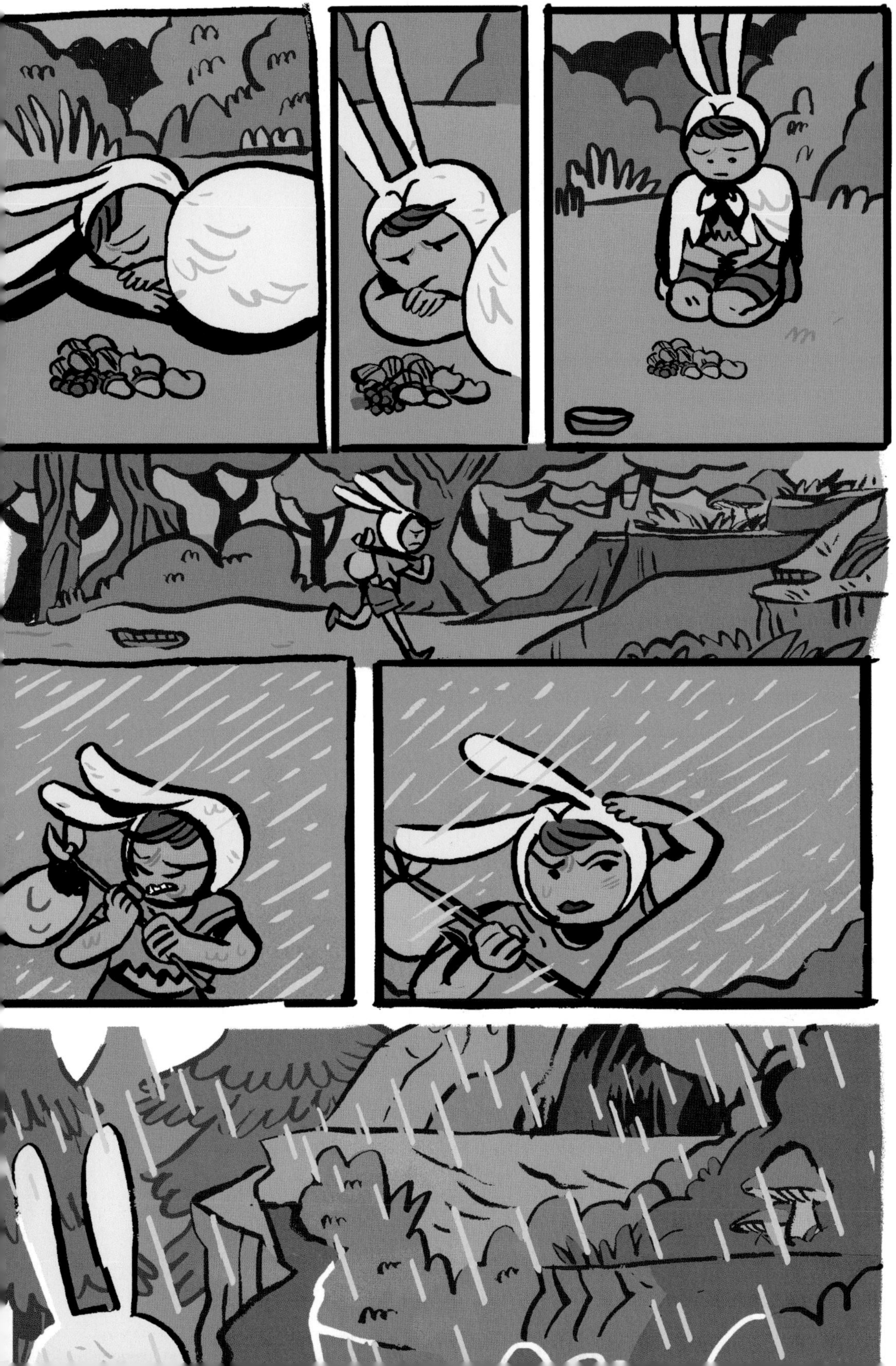

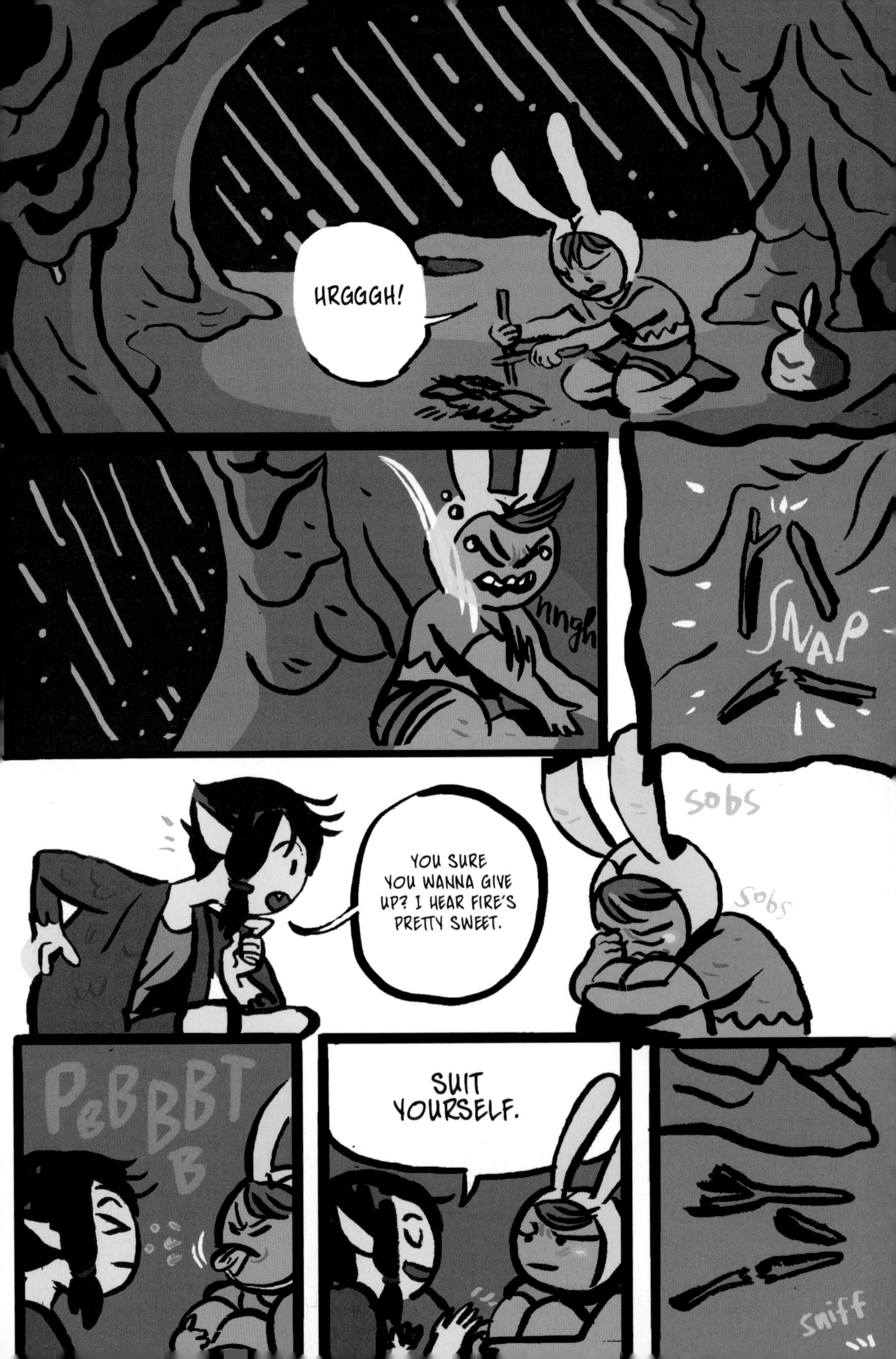
HRGGGH!
nngh
SNAP
sobs
sobs
YOU SURE YOU WANNA GIVE UP? I HEAR FIRE'S PRETTY SWEET.
PBBBBT
SUIT YOURSELF.
sniff

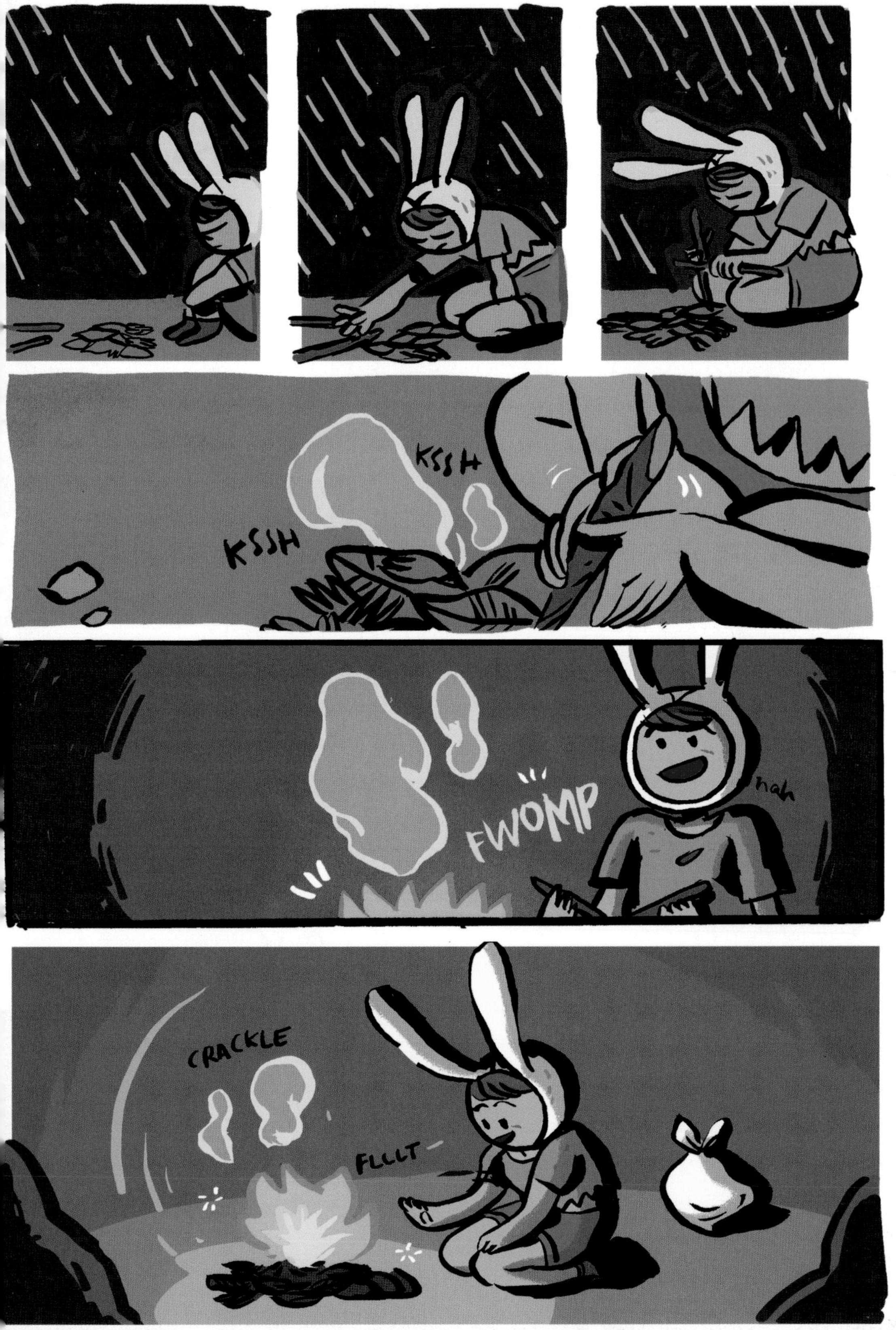
KSSH
KSSH
FWOMP
hah
CRACKLE
FLLLT

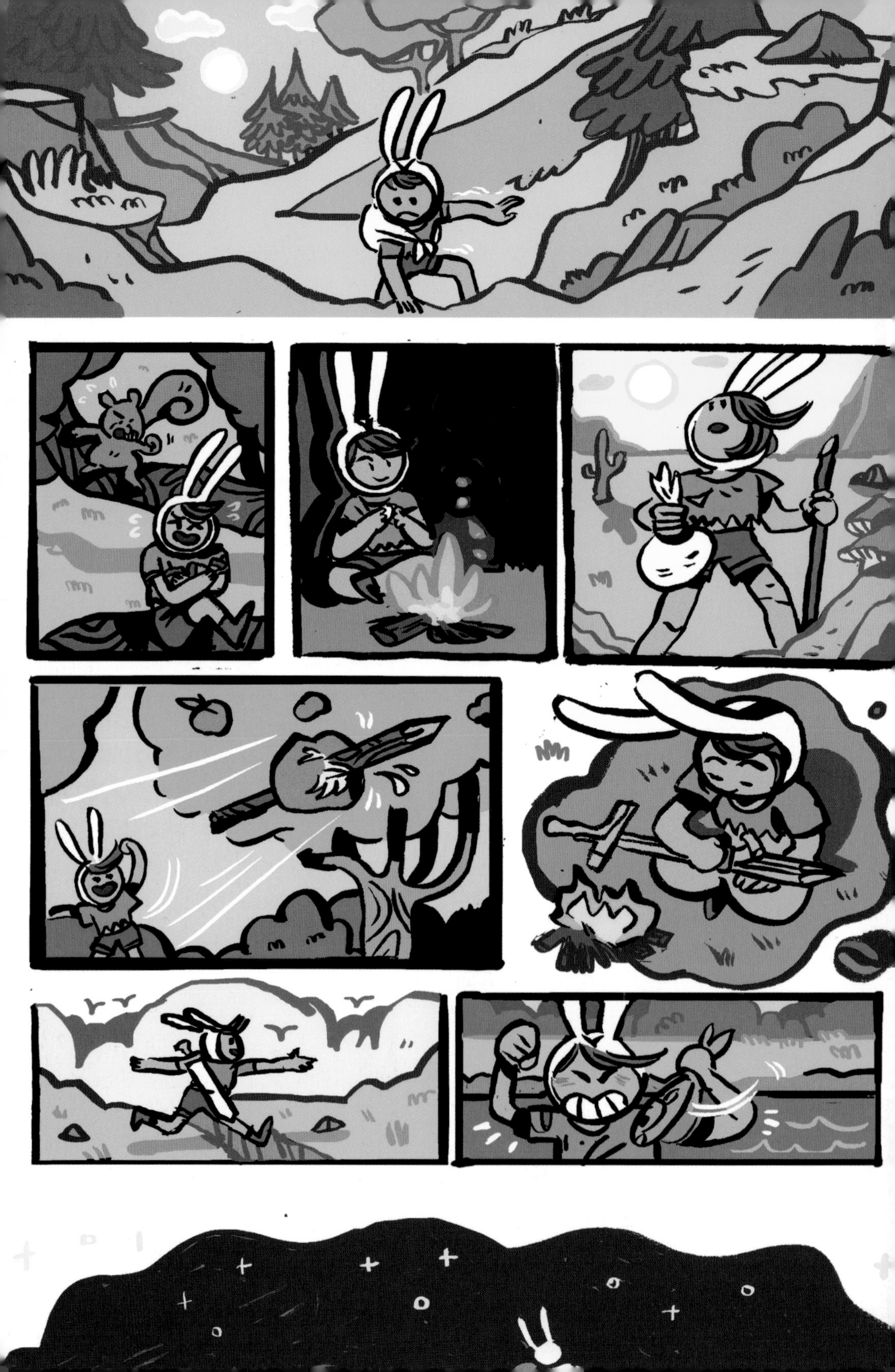

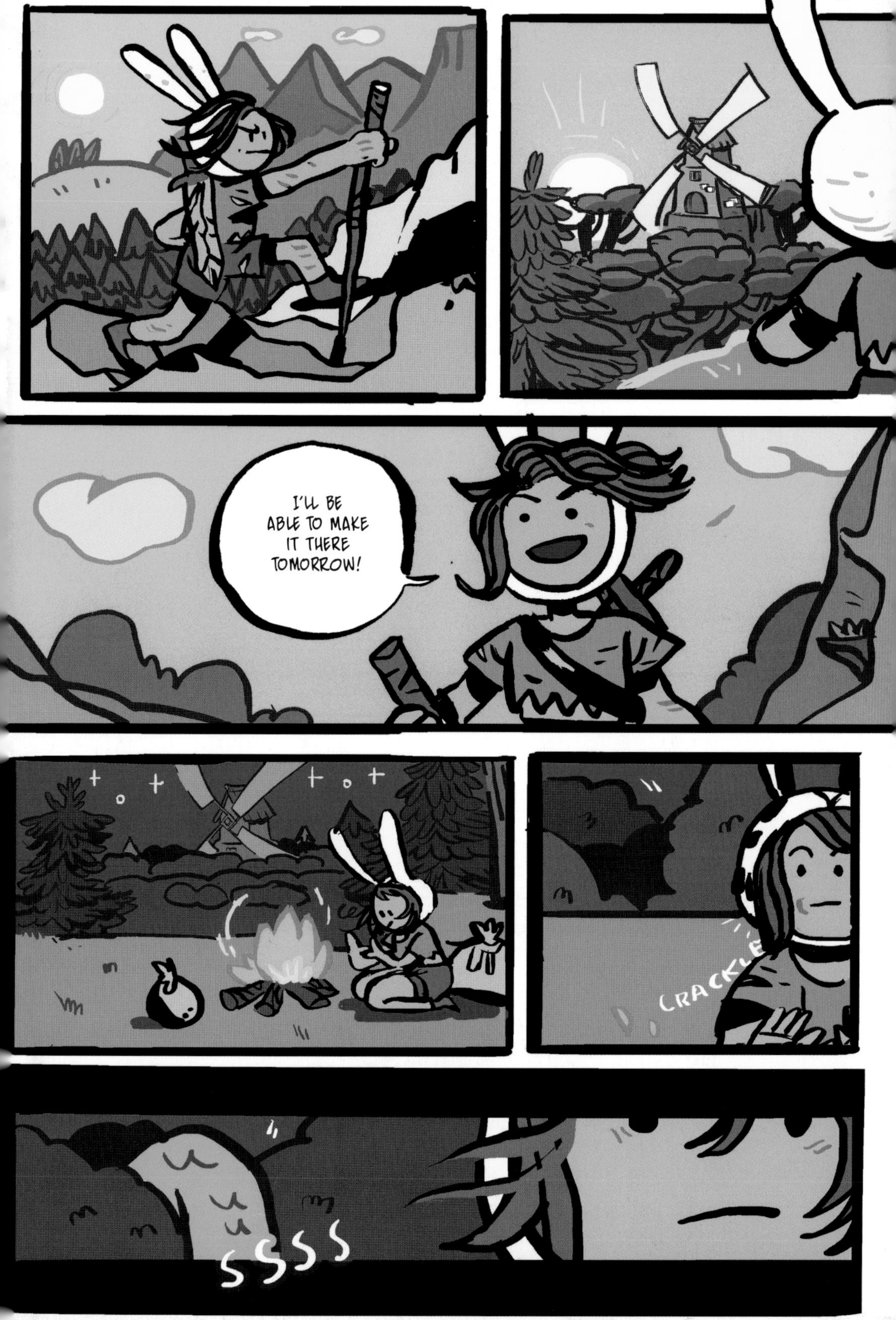
I'LL BE ABLE TO MAKE IT THERE TOMORROW!
CRACKLE
SSSS

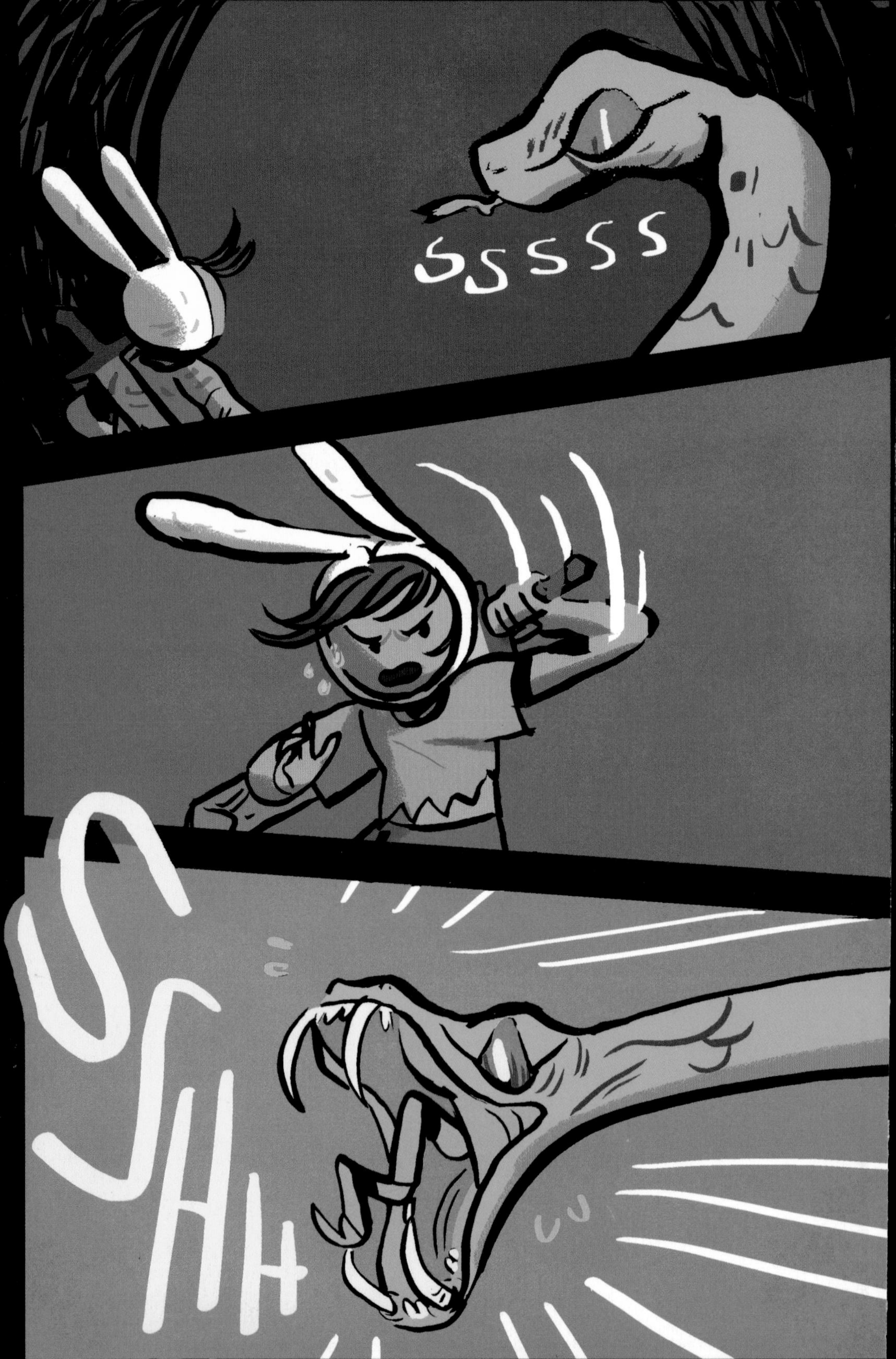

SSSSS
SSHH

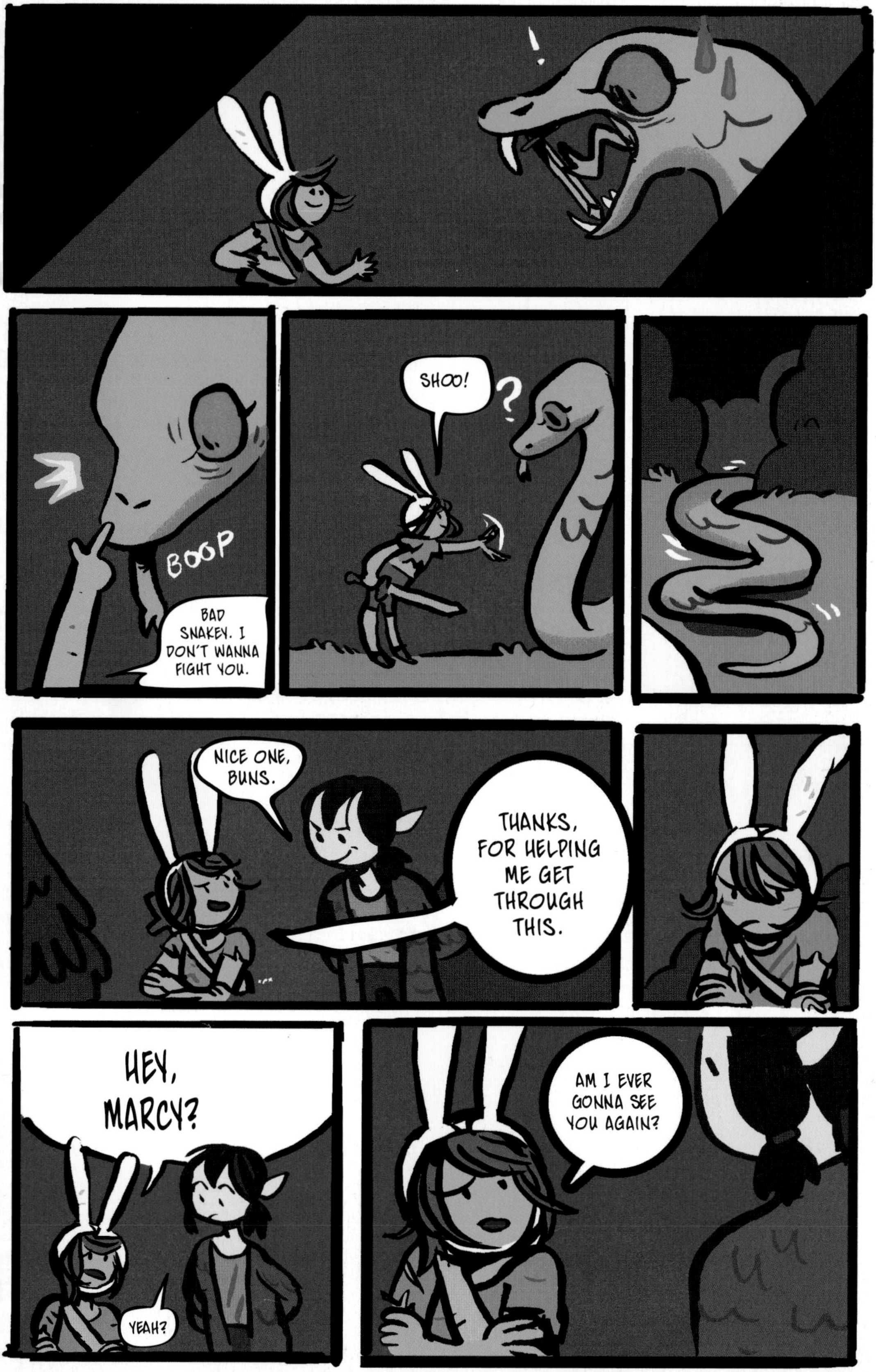
!
BOOP
BAD SNAKEY. I DON'T WANNA FIGHT YOU.
SHOO!
?
NICE ONE, BUNS.
THANKS, FOR HELPING ME GET THROUGH THIS.
HEY, MARCY?
YEAH?
AM I EVER GONNA SEE YOU AGAIN?

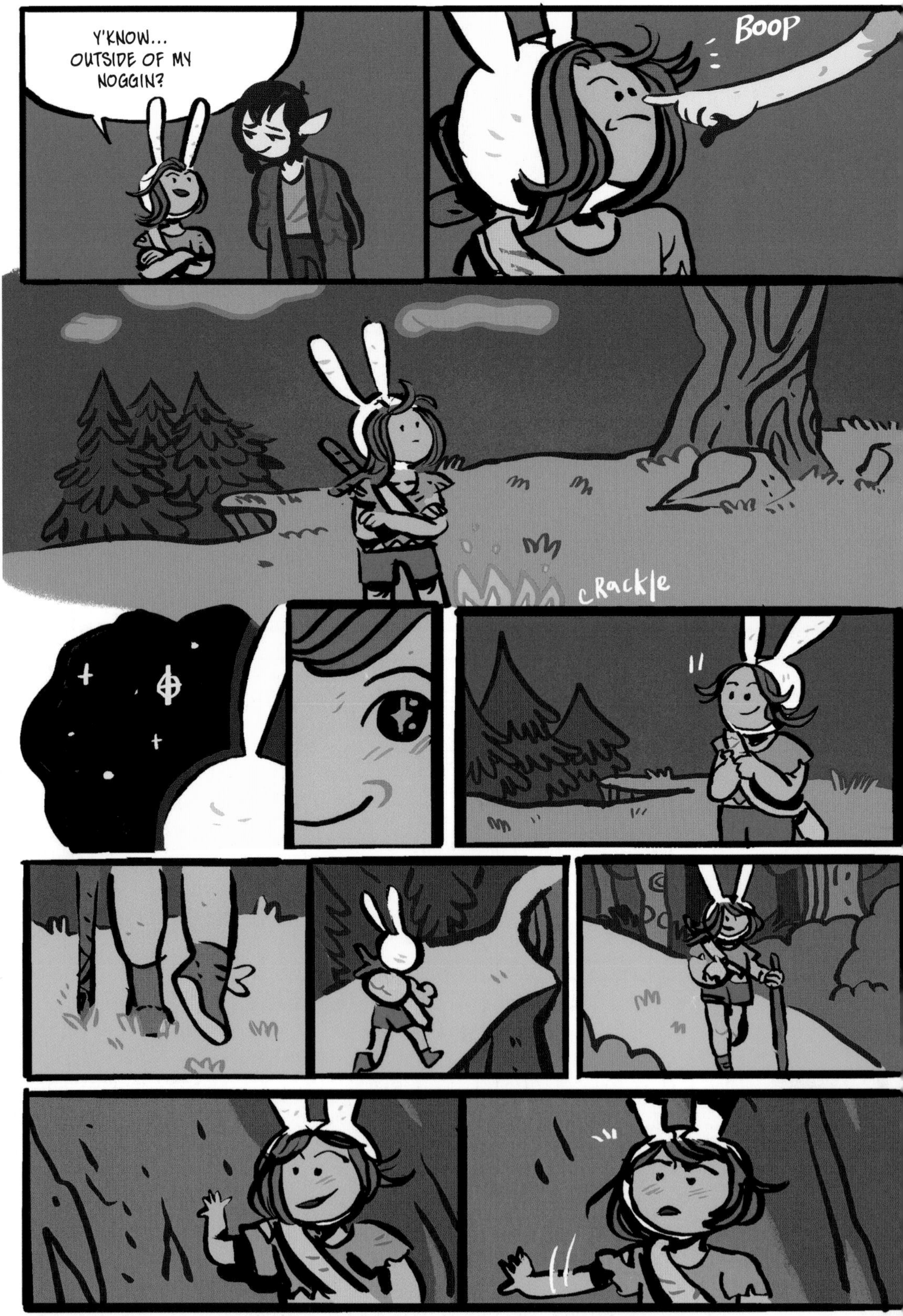
Y'KNOW...
OUTSIDE OF MY
NOGGIN?
BOOP
cRackle

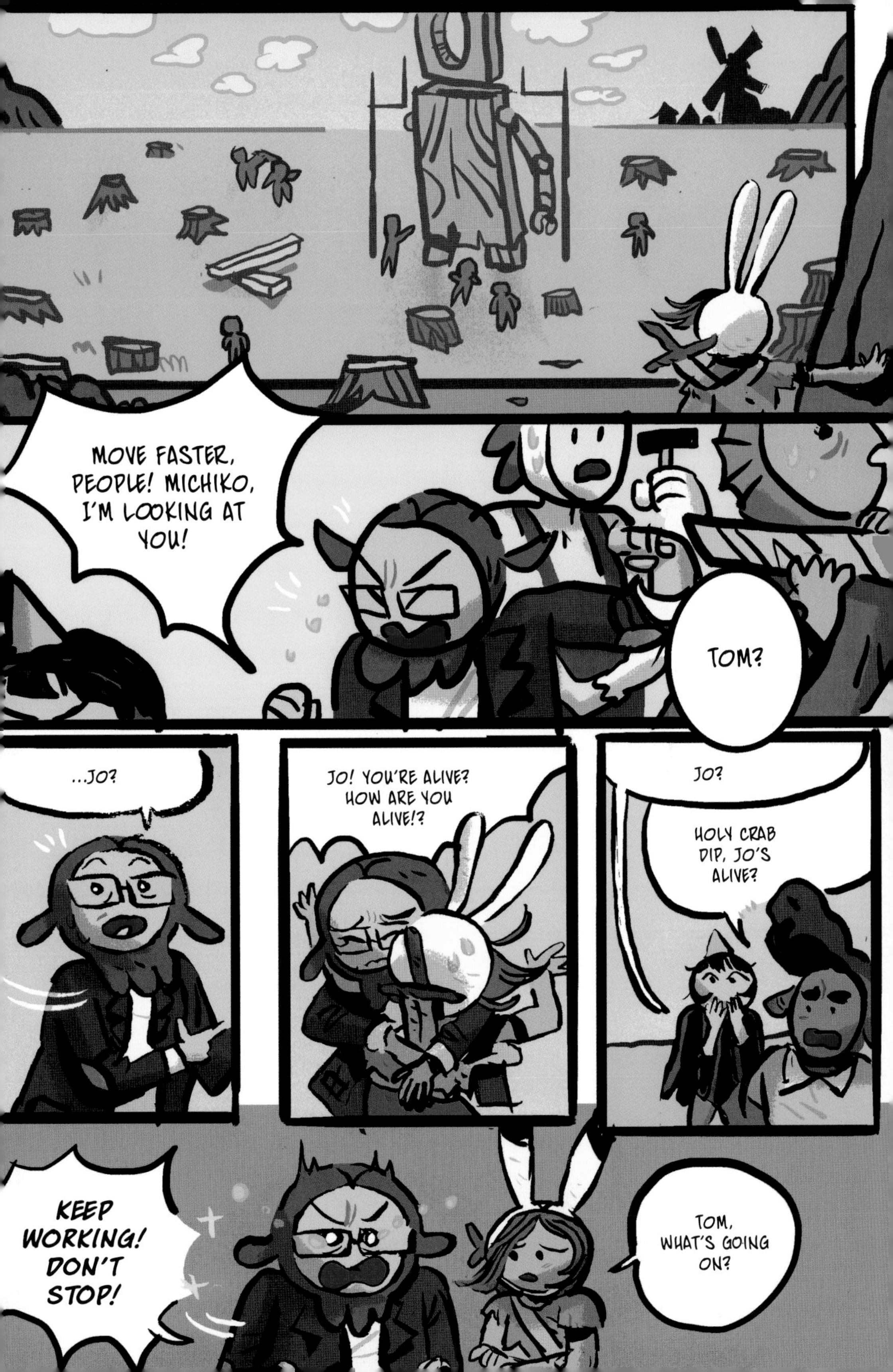
MOVE FASTER, PEOPLE! MICHIKO, I'M LOOKING AT YOU!
TOM?
...JO?
JO! YOU'RE ALIVE? HOW ARE YOU ALIVE!?
JO?
HOLY CRAB DIP, JO'S ALIVE?
KEEP WORKING! DON'T STOP!
TOM, WHAT'S GOING ON?

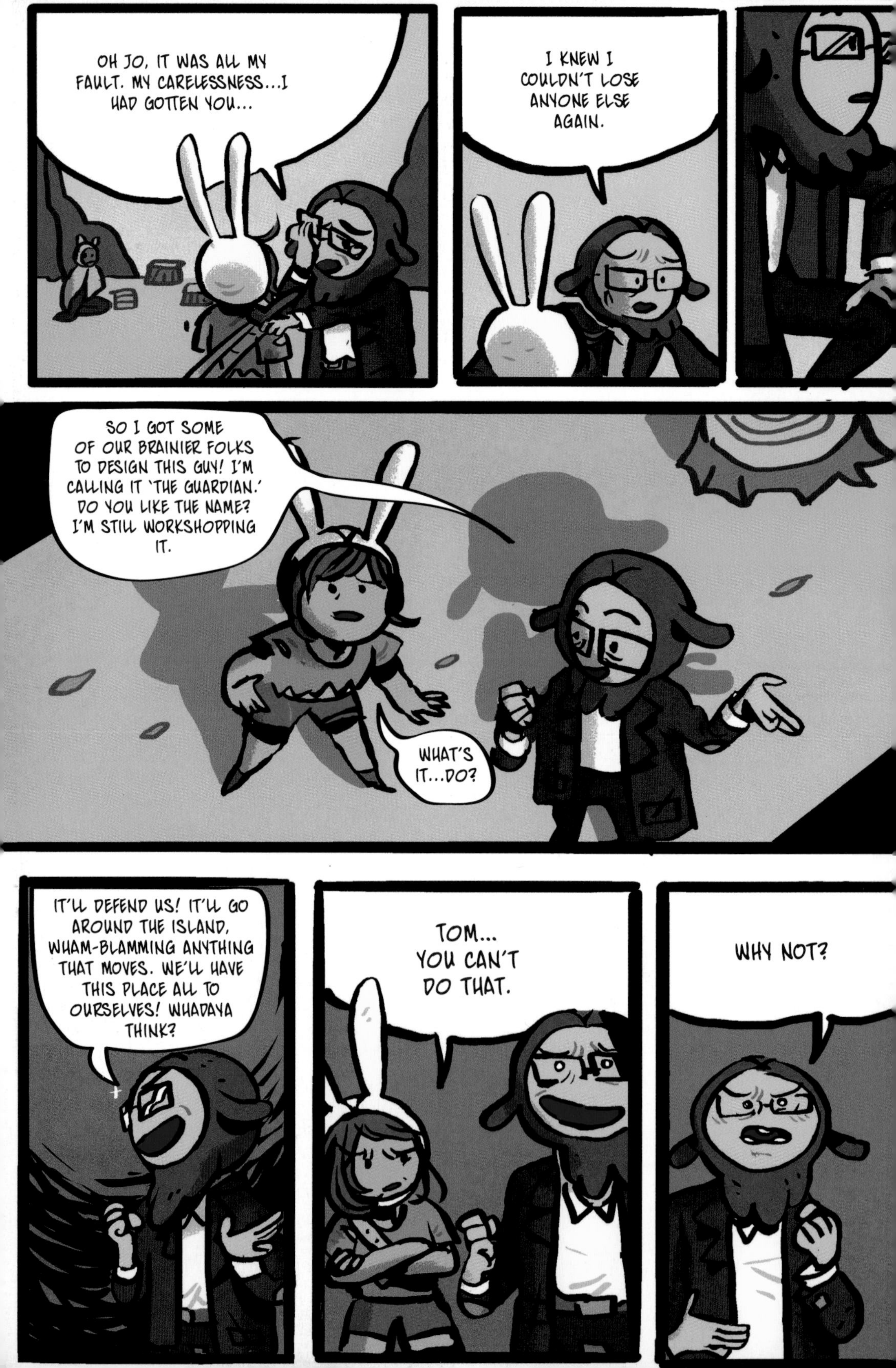
OH JO, IT WAS ALL MY FAULT. MY CARELESSNESS...I HAD GOTTEN YOU...
I KNEW I COULDN'T LOSE ANYONE ELSE AGAIN.
SO I GOT SOME OF OUR BRAINIER FOLKS TO DESIGN THIS GUY! I'M CALLING IT 'THE GUARDIAN.' DO YOU LIKE THE NAME? I'M STILL WORKSHOPPING IT.
WHAT'S IT...DO?
IT'LL DEFEND US! IT'LL GO AROUND THE ISLAND, WHAM-BLAMMING ANYTHING THAT MOVES. WE'LL HAVE THIS PLACE ALL TO OURSELVES! WHADAYA THINK?
TOM... YOU CAN'T DO THAT.
WHY NOT?

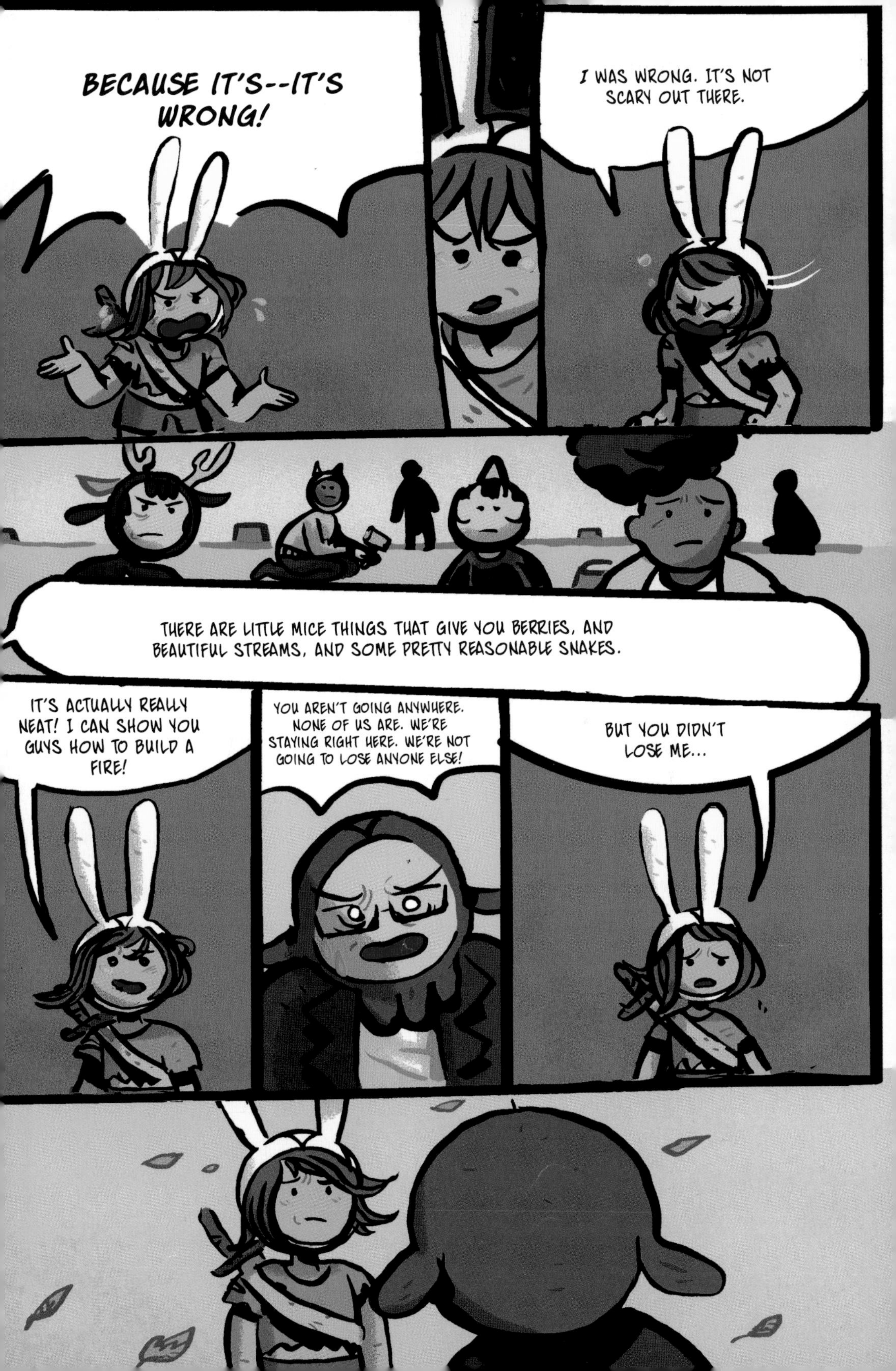
BECAUSE IT'S--IT'S WRONG!
I WAS WRONG. IT'S NOT SCARY OUT THERE.
THERE ARE LITTLE MICE THINGS THAT GIVE YOU BERRIES, AND BEAUTIFUL STREAMS, AND SOME PRETTY REASONABLE SNAKES.
IT'S ACTUALLY REALLY NEAT! I CAN SHOW YOU GUYS HOW TO BUILD A FIRE!
YOU AREN'T GOING ANYWHERE. NONE OF US ARE. WE'RE STAYING RIGHT HERE. WE'RE NOT GOING TO LOSE ANYONE ELSE!
BUT YOU DIDN'T LOSE ME...

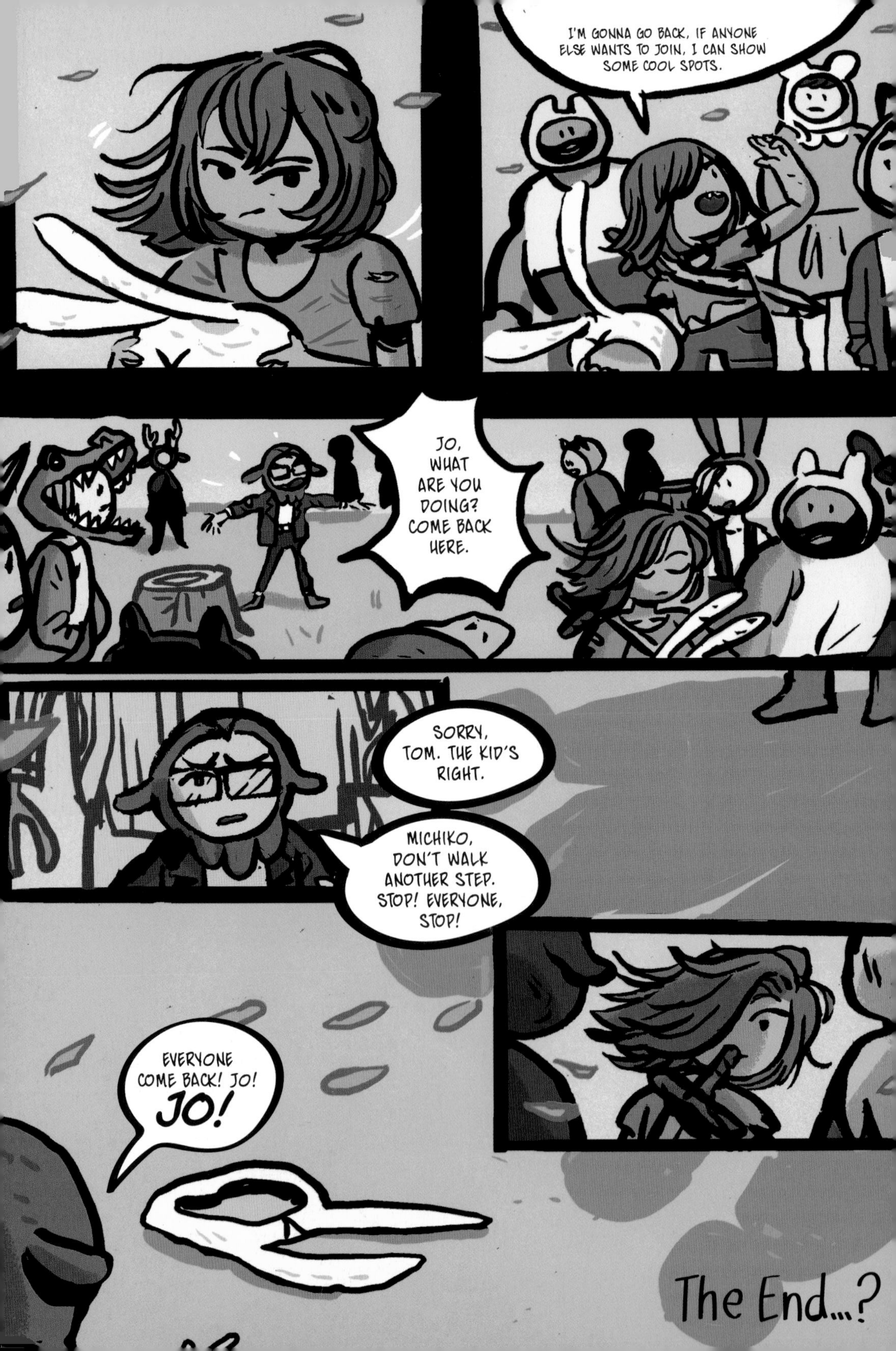
I'M GONNA GO BACK, IF ANYONE ELSE WANTS TO JOIN, I CAN SHOW SOME COOL SPOTS.
JO, WHAT ARE YOU DOING? COME BACK HERE.
SORRY, TOM. THE KID'S RIGHT.
MICHIKO, DON'T WALK ANOTHER STEP. STOP! EVERYONE, STOP!
EVERYONE COME BACK! JO! JO!
The End...?

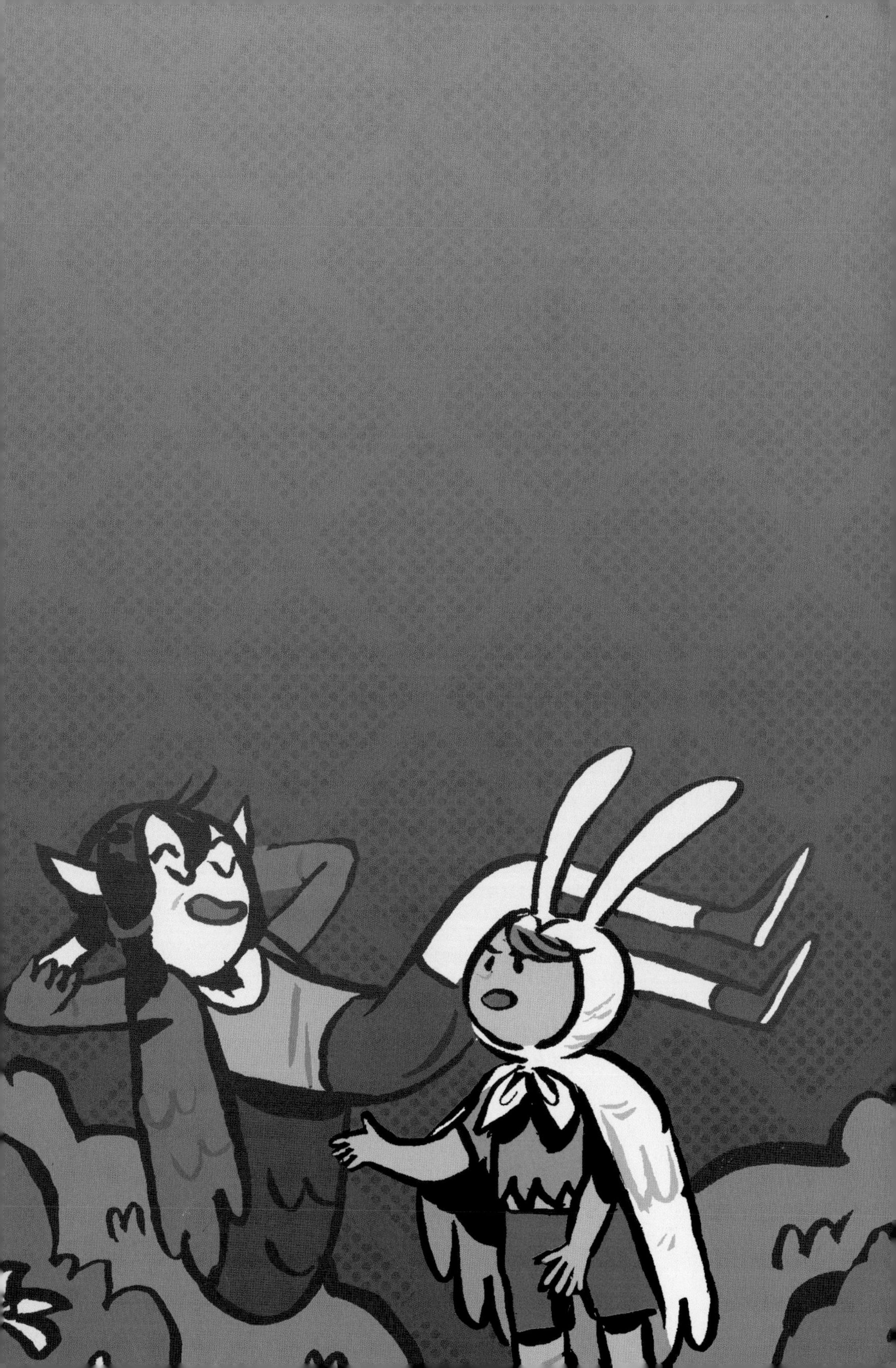

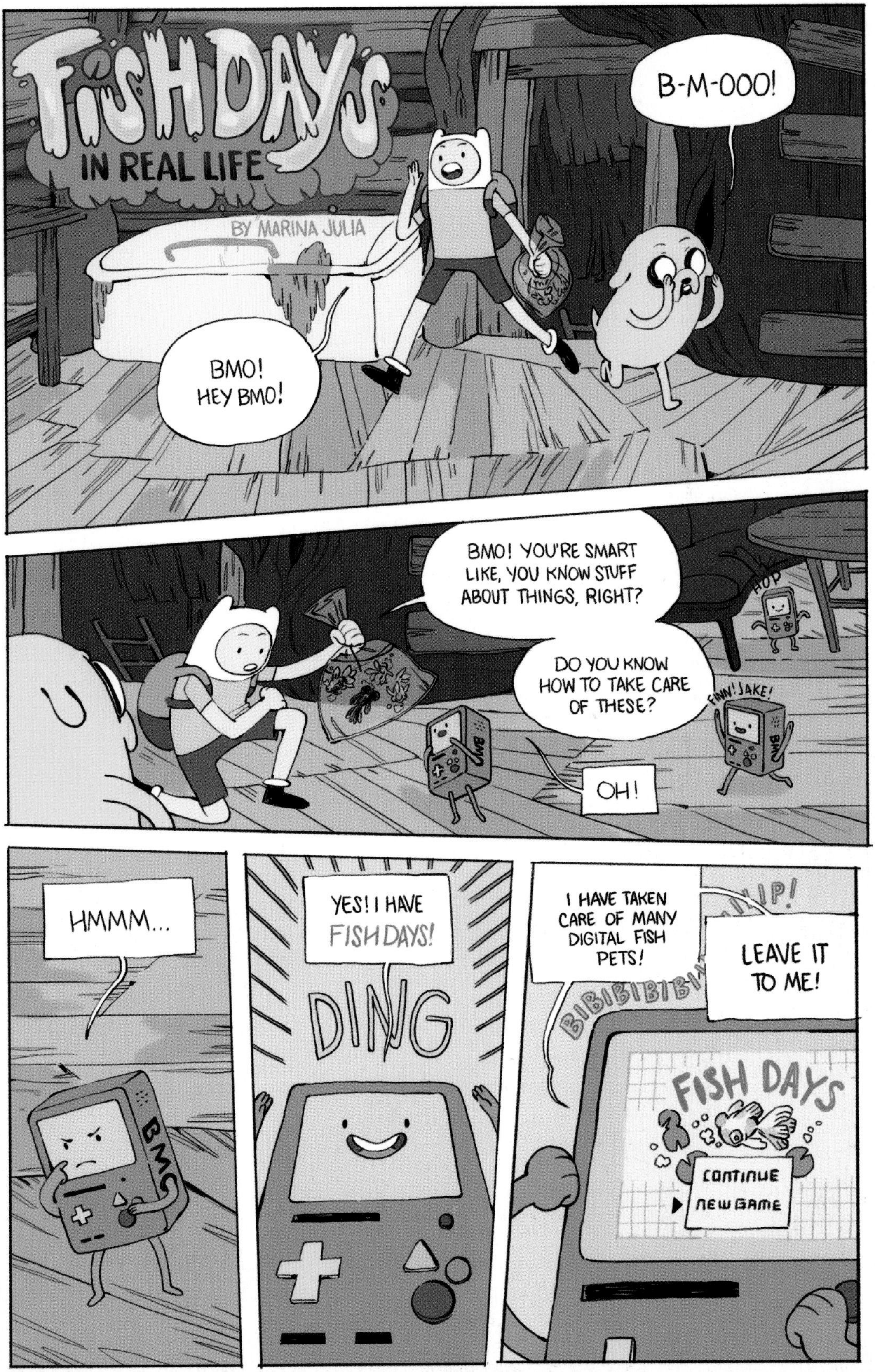
FISH DAYS
IN REAL LIFE
BY MARINA JULIA
B-M-OOO!
BMO! HEY BMO!
BMO! YOU'RE SMART LIKE, YOU KNOW STUFF ABOUT THINGS, RIGHT?
HOP
DO YOU KNOW HOW TO TAKE CARE OF THESE?
FINN! JAKE!
OH!
HMMM...
YES! I HAVE FISH DAYS!
DING
I HAVE TAKEN CARE OF MANY DIGITAL FISH PETS!
BIBIBIBIBIBI
LEAVE IT TO ME!
FISH DAYS
CONTINUE
NEW GAME

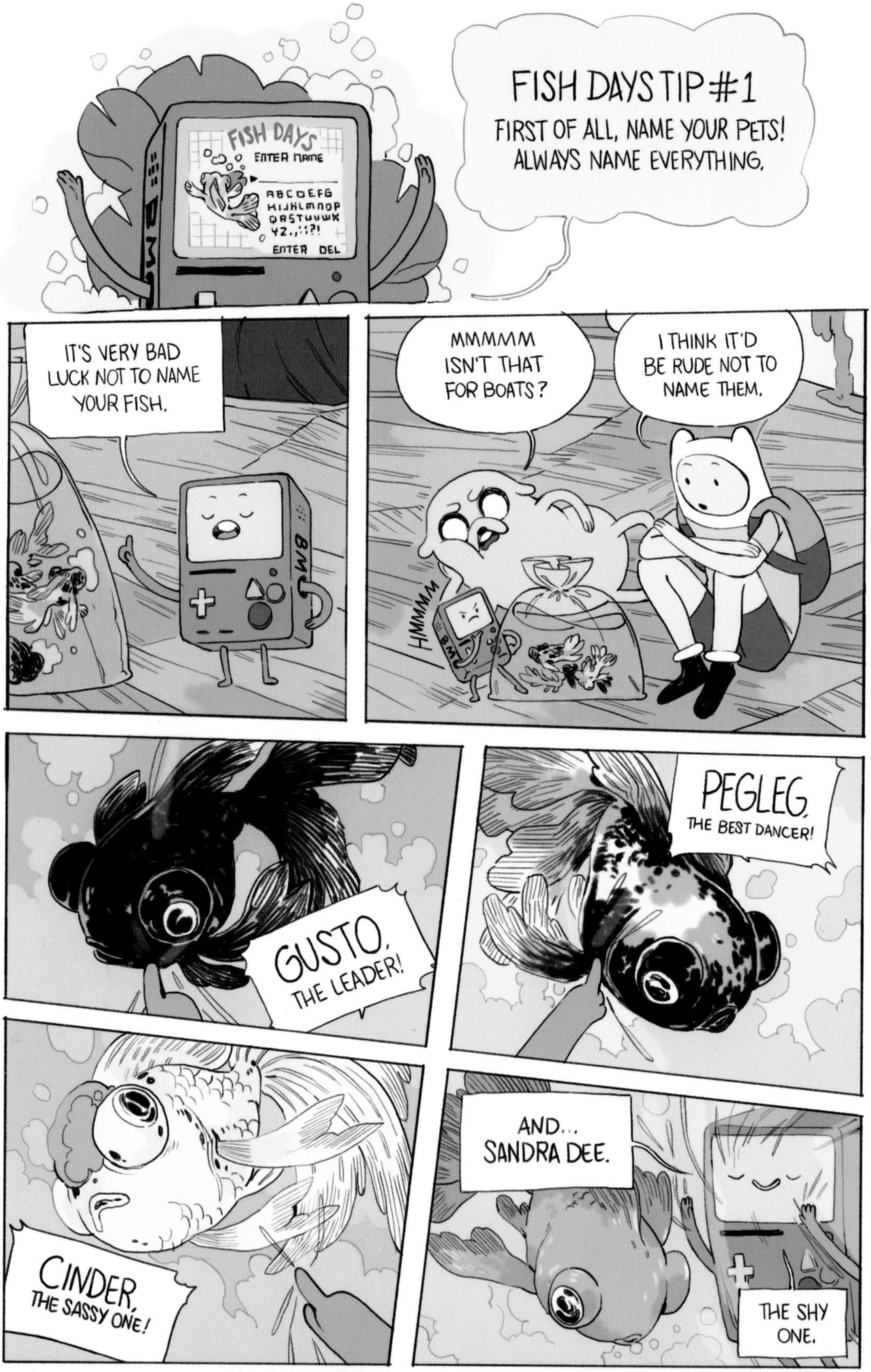
FISH DAYS
ENTER NAME
ABCDEFG
HIJKLMNOP
QRSTUVWX
YZ.,:;?!
ENTER DEL
BMO
FISH DAYS TIP #1
FIRST OF ALL, NAME YOUR PETS! ALWAYS NAME EVERYTHING.
IT'S VERY BAD LUCK NOT TO NAME YOUR FISH.
BMO
MMMMM ISN'T THAT FOR BOATS?
I THINK IT'D BE RUDE NOT TO NAME THEM.
HMMMM
BMO
GUSTO, THE LEADER!
PEGLEG, THE BEST DANCER!
CINDER, THE SASSY ONE!
AND... SANDRA DEE.
THE SHY ONE.

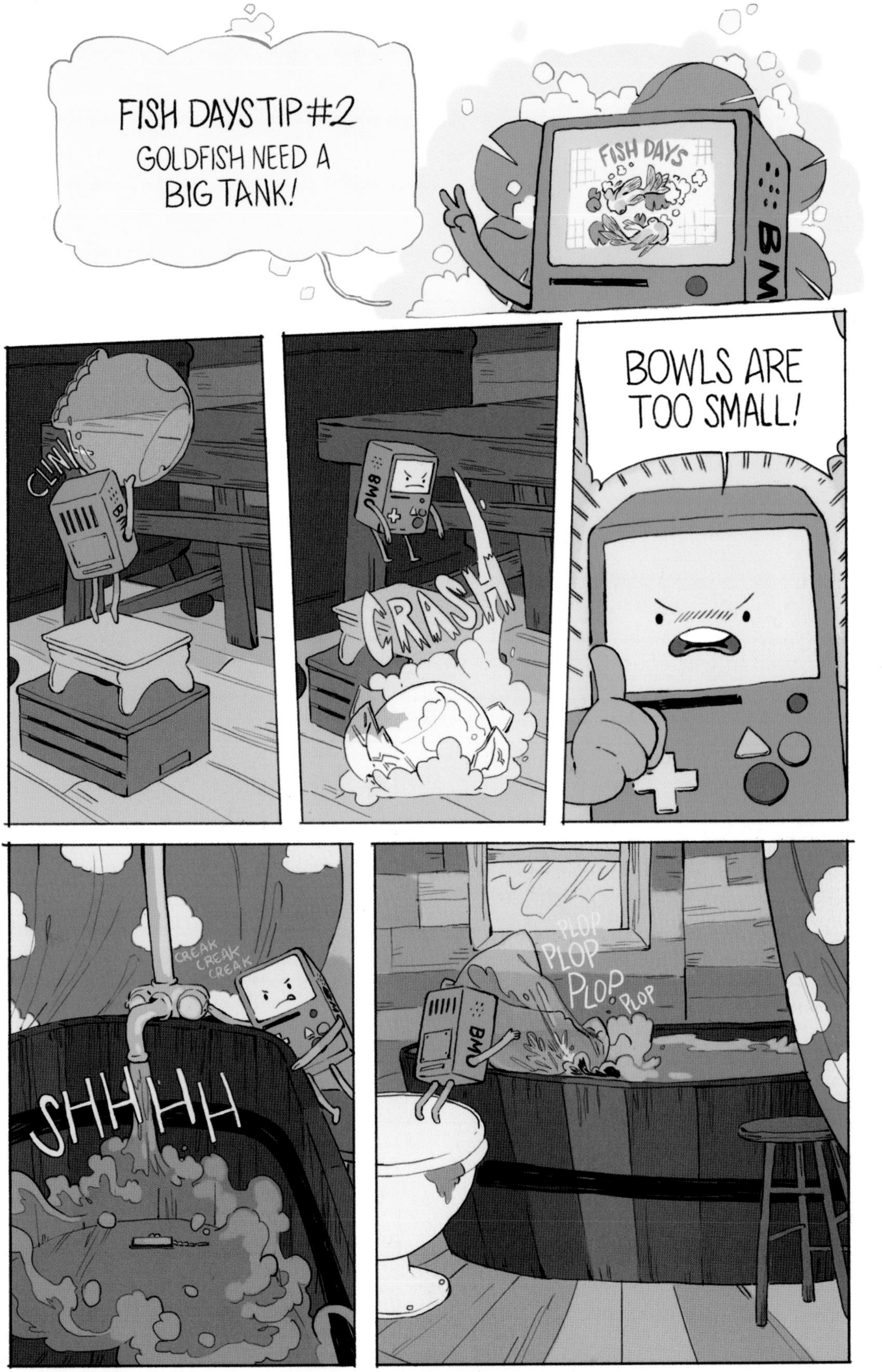
FISH DAYS TIP #2
GOLDFISH NEED A BIG TANK!
FISH DAYS
BMO
CLINK
CRASH
BOWLS ARE TOO SMALL!
CREAK CREAK CREAK
SHHHHH
PLOP PLOP PLOP PLOP

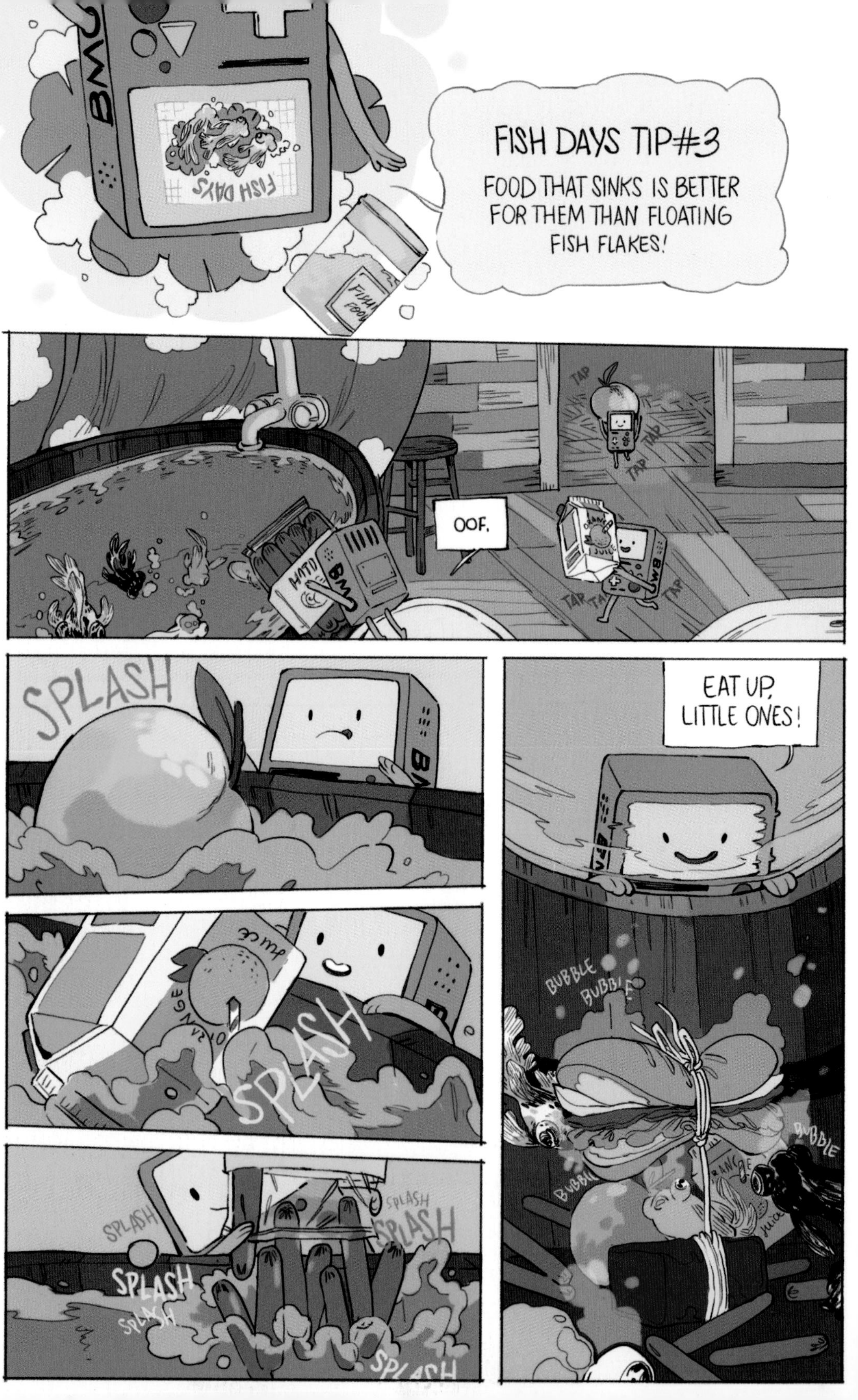
FISH DAYS TIP#3
FOOD THAT SINKS IS BETTER FOR THEM THAN FLOATING FISH FLAKES!
TAP
TAP
TAP
OOF.
TAP
TAP
TAP
SPLASH
EAT UP, LITTLE ONES!
SPLASH
SPLASH
SPLASH
SPLASH
SPLASH
SPLASH
BUBBLE
BUBBLE
BUBBLE
BUBBLE

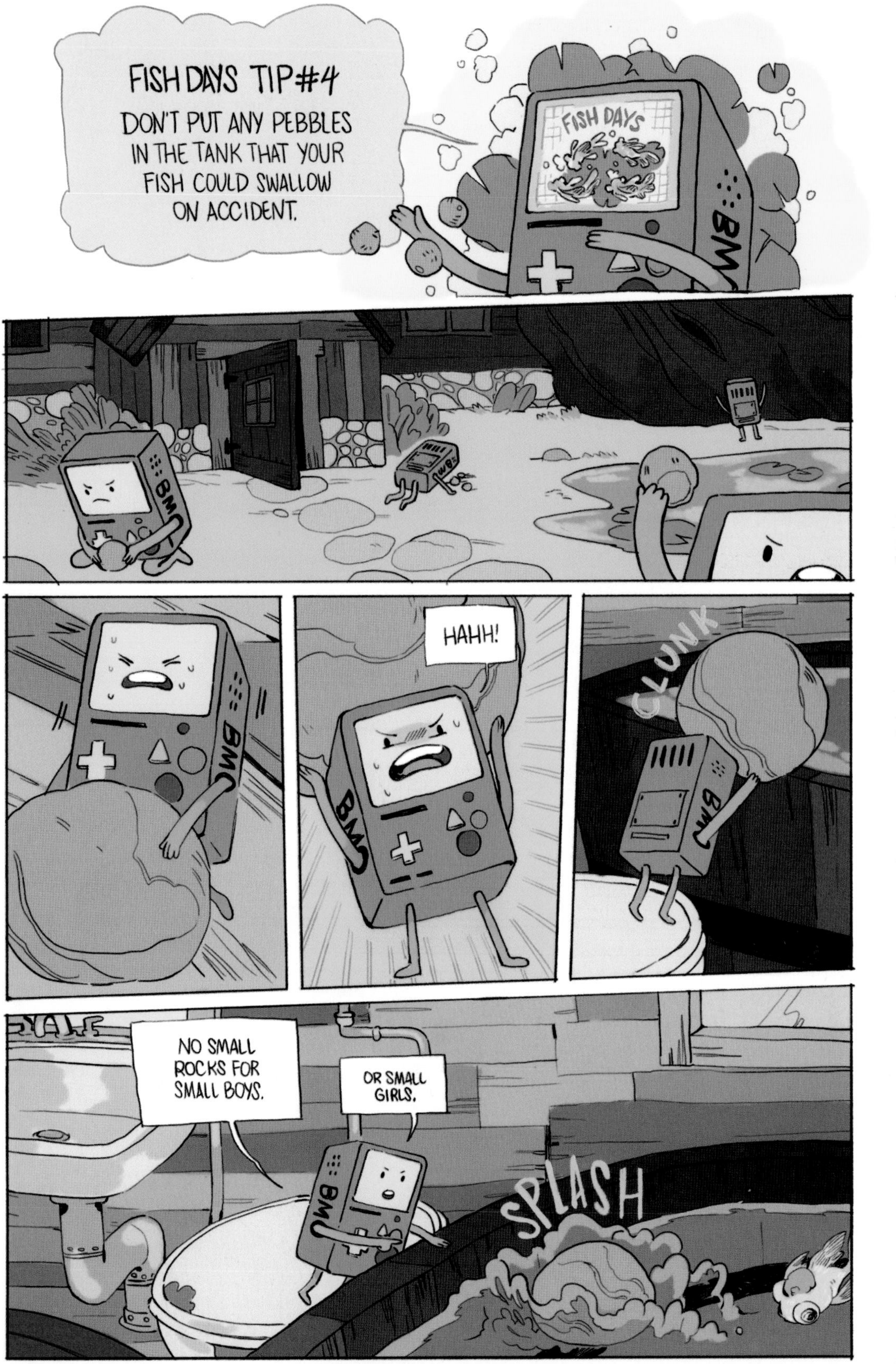
FISH DAYS TIP #4
DON'T PUT ANY PEBBLES IN THE TANK THAT YOUR FISH COULD SWALLOW ON ACCIDENT.
FISH DAYS
BMO
HAHH!
CLUNK
NO SMALL ROCKS FOR SMALL BOYS.
OR SMALL GIRLS.
SPLASH

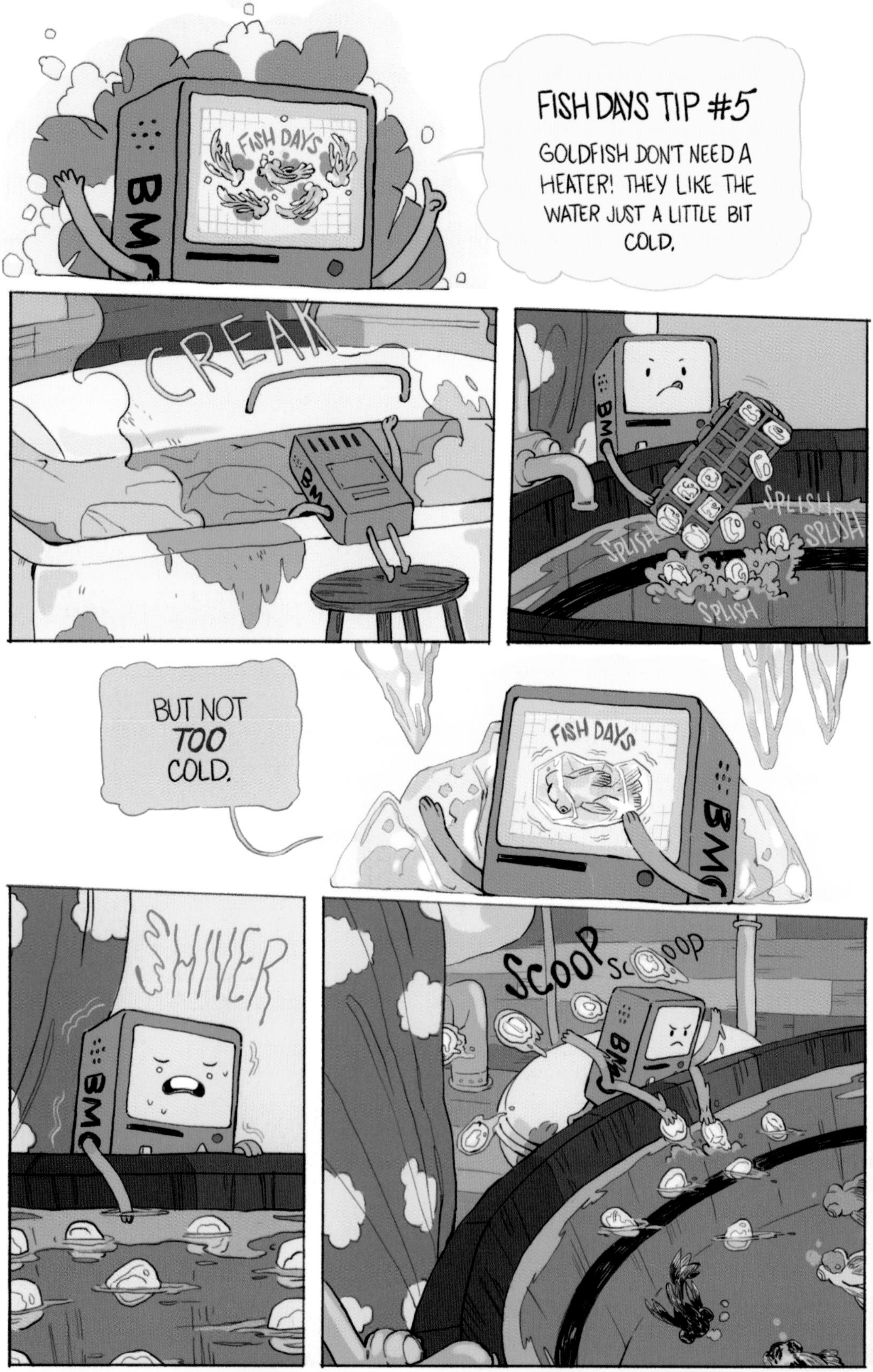
FISH DAYS
FISH DAYS TIP #5
GOLDFISH DON'T NEED A HEATER! THEY LIKE THE WATER JUST A LITTLE BIT COLD.
CREAK
SPLISH
SPLISH
SPLISH
SPLISH
FISH DAYS
BUT NOT *TOO* COLD.
SHIVER
SCOOP
SCOOP

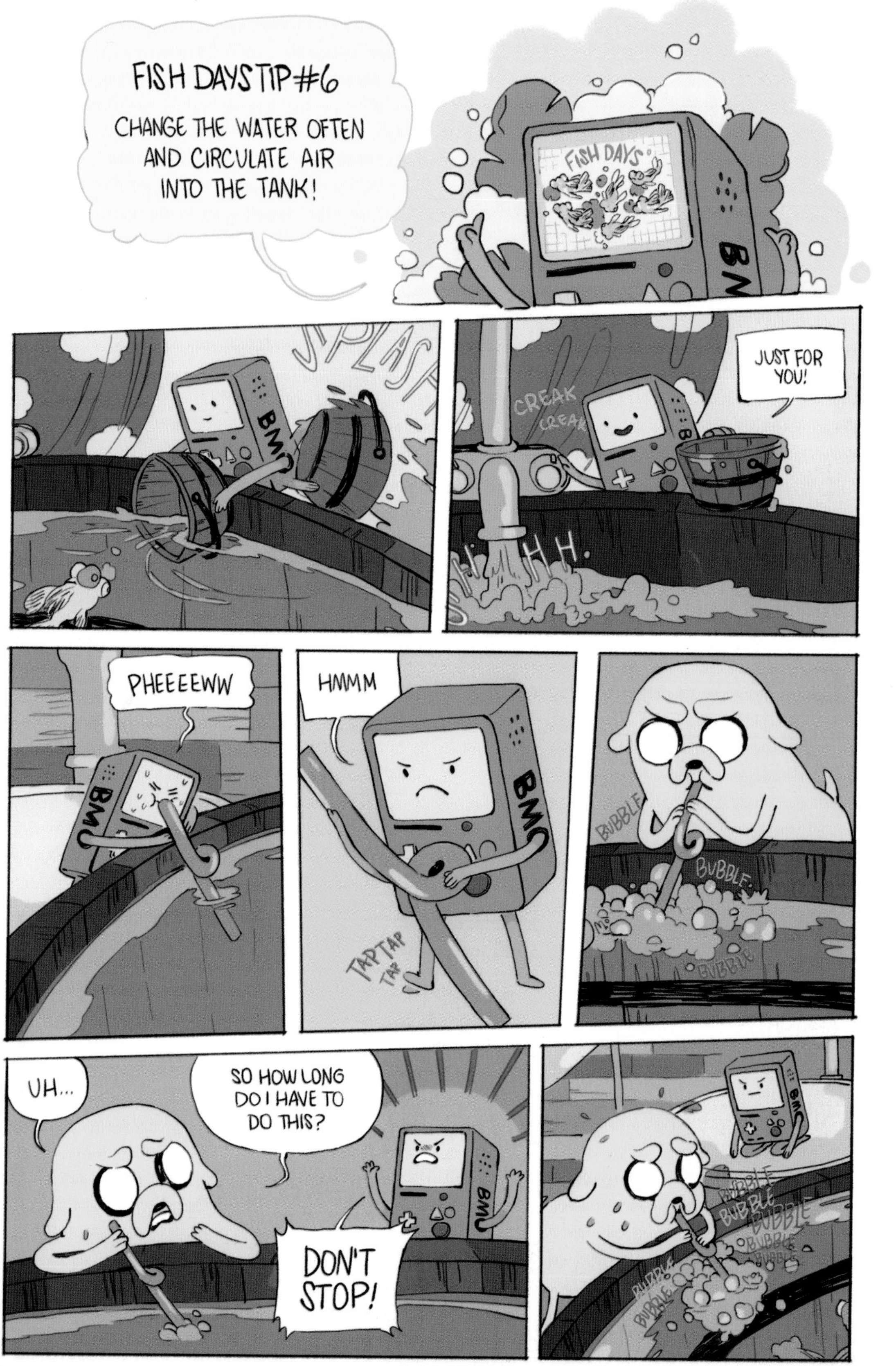

FISH DAYS TIP #6
CHANGE THE WATER OFTEN AND CIRCULATE AIR INTO THE TANK!
FISH DAYS
BMO
SPLASH
CREAK CREAK
JUST FOR YOU!
SHHH.
PHEEEEWW
HMMM
TAP TAP TAP
BUBBLE
BUBBLE.
BUBBLE
UH...
SO HOW LONG DO I HAVE TO DO THIS?
DON'T STOP!
BUBBLE BUBBLE BUBBLE BUBBLE BUBBLE
BUBBLE BUBBLE

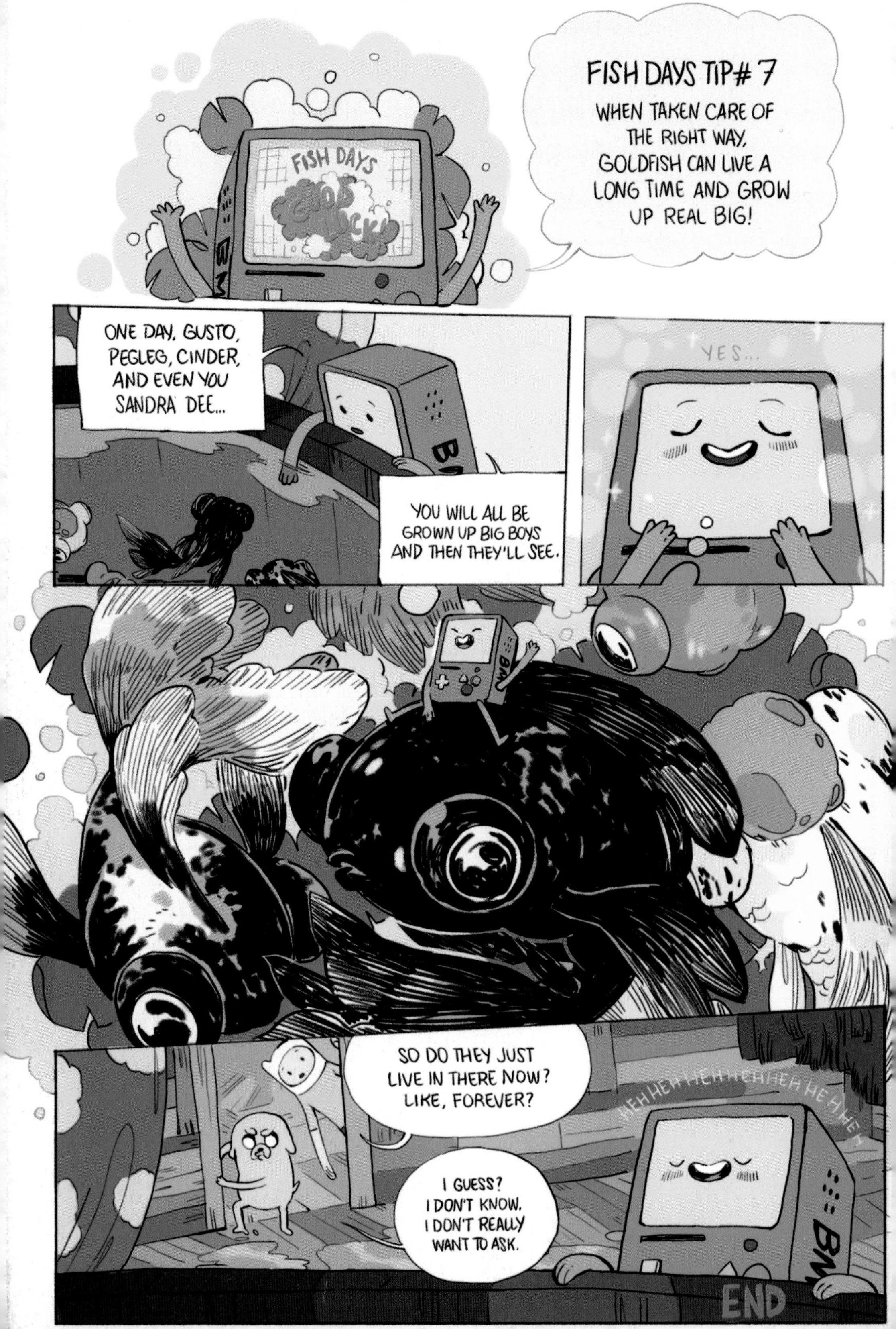
FISH DAYS
GOOD LUCK!
FISH DAYS TIP# 7
WHEN TAKEN CARE OF THE RIGHT WAY, GOLDFISH CAN LIVE A LONG TIME AND GROW UP REAL BIG!
ONE DAY, GUSTO, PEGLEG, CINDER, AND EVEN YOU SANDRA DEE...
YOU WILL ALL BE GROWN UP BIG BOYS AND THEN THEY'LL SEE.
YES...
SO DO THEY JUST LIVE IN THERE NOW? LIKE, FOREVER?
I GUESS? I DON'T KNOW. I DON'T REALLY WANT TO ASK.
HEH HEH HEH HEH HEH HEH HEH HEH HEH
END

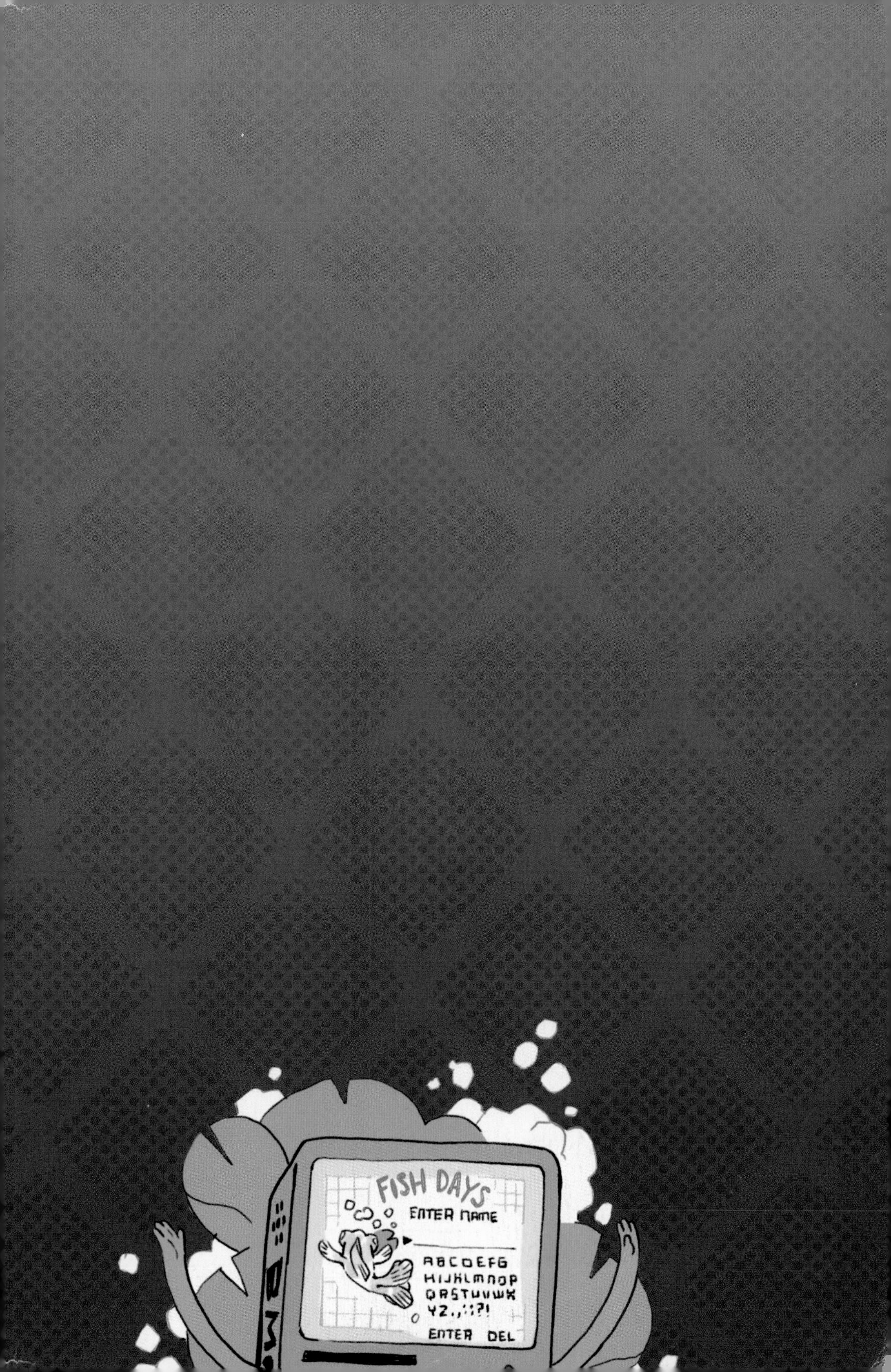
FISH DAYS
ENTER NAME
ABCDEFG
HIJKLMNOP
QRSTUVWX
YZ.,;:?!
ENTER DEL